BLACK
FROST

BOOKS BY WILLOW ROSE

BLACK FROST

WILLOW ROSE

bookouture

Published by Bookouture in 2024

An imprint of Storyfire Ltd.
Carmelite House
50 Victoria Embankment
London EC4Y 0DZ

www.bookouture.com

First published by Buoy Media LLC in 2020.

ISBN: 978-1-83525-345-8
eBook ISBN: 978-1-83525-344-1

This book is a work of fiction. Names, characters, businesses, organisations,
places and events other than those clearly in the public domain, are either the
product of the author's imagination or are used fictitiously. Any resemblance to
actual persons, living or dead, events or locales is entirely coincidental.

CONTENT NOTE

This book features graphic scenes of violence. If this is
potentially sensitive to you, please read with care.

PROLOGUE
FANOE ISLAND, DENMARK

It wasn't easy to do a Wiccan ritual in the outdoors. Tanja had done many indoors, but never really succeeded at doing one outside. She had been so certain that tonight was the right night. It was a full moon, yet the cloud cover made it impossible even to see it. The weather forecast had said clear skies all night, but she should have known better than to trust that. Living on Fanoe island in the Wadden Sea in Denmark, the weather more than often acted like an angsty teenager. It was so unreliable.

Tanja had asked her coven of five other girls to meet her in the park downtown at ten o'clock. But now, as they were sitting there in a circle, the altar set up in front of them, the moon was hiding behind the clouds again, and the wind kept blowing out the candles.

"Hurry up," Nina said and rubbed her hands together, then breathed on them to warm them. "It's freezing."

"I'm working on it," Tanja said, then lit the five candles again. She stared at them angrily, hoping they'd stay lit now. Yet seconds later, a gust of wind puffed in on them, and they were blown out again.

"Argh!" Tanja groaned, annoyed. She rubbed her thighs to

try to get the blood flowing through them. Then she looked at her friends, the girls in the coven, who were all just sitting there on the frozen ground.

Maybe doing a skyclad ritual wasn't the best idea, she thought.

Her bare skin was starting to hurt in the biting cold. And it wasn't just the frost they had to fight; there was also the matter of dog walkers coming by every few minutes, making sure their dogs relieved themselves before bedtime. Seeing six naked teenage girls in a clearing on the frozen ground could raise some eyebrows in their small community. Not to mention the fact that their parents had no idea what they were doing, and on a small island like this, they were almost sure to be recognized by someone who knew them.

"Are we done soon?" Ingrid asked, her teeth chattering. "I don't like it out here this late. My parents would kill me if they knew where I was."

Tanja grumbled, annoyed at her. Ingrid was always such a wimpy kid. She almost regretted having brought her. But she felt sorry for her, and she needed that last member to complete the coven, so she had accepted her anyway when she asked. But, of course, the girl would cause nothing but trouble with all her complaining.

Yet Tanja wasn't giving up just like that. She didn't carry all this stuff, the water, the incense, the charcoal, the chalice, and the cider all the way to the park just to give up. It was pretty hard to carry it all by herself without spilling the water and shaking up the cider. Setting up everything had taken forever too. She wasn't going to pack it all up and go home so quickly just because Ingrid couldn't stand a little cold.

Tanja tried once more to light the candles and succeeded. She waited for a few seconds, and as there was no gust of wind to blow them out, she finally smiled. Her teeth were rattling, yes, but she was smiling.

"All right," she said and grabbed her friends' hands in hers.

She began chanting, calling the elements to be present, and the others soon chimed in. They called on the four elements—earth, fire, water, and air—the elements that serve as guardians and protectors of the Wiccan. It felt like a warmth spread among them, and it suddenly didn't seem as unpleasant as it had in the beginning.

Being nude was such an essential part of them feeling close to nature that she had insisted they do it, even though they would be freezing. It brought them closer to the divine, the goddess. It also provided them with a sense of freedom and power from being without the confines of clothing. It was all just limitations the world placed on them to keep them from connecting with nature.

As the—self-appointed—high priestess of their coven, Tanja had decided it was time for them to set themselves free. Here they were, as vulnerable as when they were just born, yet stronger than ever. It was time for them to reunite themselves with their inner strength, with nature, the universe, and other beings.

The ritual became a success. At least for a little while. The girls chanted, they danced, and Tanja walked around the circle with the amulet. As she had made the entire three-hundred-sixty degrees around it, she tossed the amulet inside the ring, while whispering into the night, "the moon's end."

As she did this, she paused and stared, waiting for the deity to show herself, for the energies to rise inside the circle and fill them all with her strong presence. Tanja was barely moving as she waited with bated breath.

The candle lights flickered before they were all blown out at the same time.

Tanja gasped.

"Did we succeed?" Nina asked. "Did we do it? Is she here? Is the goddess here? Has she blessed us with her presence?"

"I... I think so," Tanja said and stared into the circle at the altar they had made when the moon decided to peek out just enough to light up the clearing.

"I think I can feel her," Nina said, her voice relieved and blissful. She burst into laughter, then stood to her feet and started to turn. She was dancing in a circle, reaching out her arms.

"I think she's here. I feel her."

Tanja wasn't sure she felt anything, and it annoyed her immensely. If Nina did, then she should be able to as well, shouldn't she? She was, after all, the high priestess, the most devoted. She should feel the goddess's presence before any of the others. Tanja stepped inside the circle and stood by the altar, then grabbed the chalice between her hands.

"We must thank her."

Just as she lifted the chalice up toward the sky and chanted the words from her spell book that she had spent so much time memorizing, the moon disappeared again, and the clearing fell into deep darkness.

Ingrid gulped nervously and took a step back, away from the circle. Ignoring this and deciding that next time she'd bring someone else instead of Ingrid, Tanja closed her eyes. She focused on visualizing the goddess while she took the chalice and drank from it.

That's when she felt it. It was like there was a massive burst of energy flowing inside the circle. It was stronger than anything she had ever felt before. Tanja was almost overwhelmed and didn't think about cold or frostbite or chattering teeth anymore. The energy from the deity they were trying to summon warmed her and made her feel at such deep peace with herself. She felt uplifted, almost like she was levitating, and she began dancing, feeling lightheaded, like she was defying gravity itself. Finally, she sensed her. Finally, the goddess blessed her with her presence and her unlimited energy.

It felt amazing.

Tanja laughed almost manically and danced and chanted loudly but was forcefully pulled out of her trance when Nina suddenly spoke, her voice smothered in concern.

"W-where is Ingrid?"

Tanja opened her eyes, and just like that, the feeling was gone; the energy was sucked right out of the circle, much to her great disappointment.

"What do you mean, where is Ingrid?" she almost hissed.

"She's not here," Nina said, turning her head to look. "She was there just a minute ago."

Tanja put the chalice down, then looked in the direction of where Ingrid had been standing. It was empty like Nina had said. There was no sign of Ingrid. Tanja looked around them, turning in circles.

"Ingrid?" she called, alarm rising inside of her. "Ingrid? INGRID?"

PART I
ONE WEEK LATER

ONE

"Emma, I know you mean well, but I have to stop now. This is getting out of hand. There's no more I can do."

I stared at my lawyer, Michael, sitting on the other side of the table. His sparse hair on top of his head was slicked back against his scalp, making it look like he had more hair left than he really did. We had agreed to meet at Café Mimosa over brunch to discuss my case. Or, as my lawyer would put it, the lack of one.

"But they have the girl," I said. "I know they took Skye, and they're keeping her there. They kidnapped her right out of my home."

"Omicon is refusing that they have any knowledge of her, and because we can't prove she even exists, it's kind of difficult to—"

I slammed my palm onto the table, and our coffee cups clattered. Michael gave me a wide stare.

"But they do have her. And I want her back."

I pulled out my phone and showed him a picture of Skye. I hadn't seen her in seven months and had tried everything. I had reported Omicon to the police, claiming they kidnapped her, and Morten had been considerate enough to look into the possibility of them searching the facility. Still, their expensive lawyers had blocked every effort. Morten and I were no longer an item, so as the days passed and I kept showing up, asking if there was news, he had started to brush me off. Now, I was getting desperate.

"There you go. Isn't that proof enough that she exists?" I asked, pointing at Skye's picture. "She's very real. This is a girl's life we're talking about."

I was barely breathing; that's how angry I was. I had grown to love Skye, even though I didn't know anything about her. She had come into my son's life when he found her in our garden. She fell from a treetop one day, and that's why he had named her Skye. Because she sort of fell from the sky.

Victor, my son, wasn't an easy child and rarely made friends. But Skye made him get out of that shell of his, and they had a special bond, one unlike anything I had ever seen. They were weird together, yes, did strange things, like communicating in ways that didn't need words, and Skye taught Victor to make things levitate, like utensils and stuff, but I had never seen my son as happy as when he was with her.

Where she came from soon became less important. She didn't speak, so she couldn't tell me, and no one missed her. So, I had kept her for some time, till she one day suddenly disappeared from Victor's room at night, and I spotted big sets of boots in the snow outside the next morning. I knew who had taken her; they had tried to get into my house before while asking for the girl, and even became violent toward me at one point.

They were goons sent by Omicon, a company outside of town, with scientists who officially researched new medicine for diabetes patients, but never had any results to show for it. I suspected they were the ones who had kept Skye and done experiments on her, just like they had done on Lyn. She was a woman I had gotten to know when she came through the pipes to my house to look for her son, Daniel.

Both of them were a sort of water creature who could look both human and then dissolve into a water-like substance. Just like the old vampire, Samuel, who had dated my daughter for a little while. He lived off the green blood in children like my son —they all came from another place, another world similar to ours, connected by the sewers under our island. They had been sent here because of a terrible war in their own world, Lyn had told me, but I didn't know a lot of details. Only that they entered through the sewers and ended up in the pipes at the mental institution, Fishy Pines, where a plumber pulled them out before he was murdered.

It was the same place where my son was now going to school because of his social challenges. The part of the building where the creatures had entered was currently closed off, and the building condemned. I was certain there was a connection to Omicon and that they were doing awful things there, in the place that Lyn's son, Daniel referred to as "The place where no one hears you scream."

Daniel was living with me for the time being, as I had promised his mother Lyn to keep him safe until she could get them both out of here, back to where they really belonged. It was seven months ago that I made her that promise, and I hadn't seen her since. It was all quite a strange story. I was certain I didn't know the half of it, and maybe I never would. But I did understand that Skye was gone and probably in great danger.

Michael rubbed his face. I knew he was getting tired of me, but I wasn't going to let this go. They had taken this girl and kidnapped her from my house, and I wasn't going to accept that I couldn't do anything about it.

"She isn't in the system, Emma. Social services has never heard about her, she has never been registered in any schools, and no one is missing her. No parents, no foster families, and no children's homes are searching for her. I have looked everywhere. I've been sending the pictures you gave me everywhere, to anyone who might know something, but no one has ever seen her before or heard about her, so it's hard to get a judge to side with you and give us a court order. We can't get in there, Emma. I've tried everything. I have other clients I need to attend to. These past several months, I have prioritized you and your case, but to tell you the truth, I don't think it is possible."

My eyes grew wide, and I stopped chewing on the bacon I had just put in my mouth.

"Not possible? What do you mean not possible?"

He grabbed my hands in his. Mine were greasy from the bacon, but he didn't seem to notice.

"You have to give up, Emma."

I pulled my hands out of his. "Give up? What do you mean give up? I can't let them kidnap a girl and not try to stop them. Victor is driving me crazy about this. He misses her so much; it's tearing him apart. I can hardly get him to go to school in the mornings, and once he gets back, he goes out into the garden and just sits there in the snow, looking up at the tree where he found her like he's expecting her to fall from the sky again. It's unbearable."

Michael sighed. I could tell he had already left me in his mind and was thinking about his other cases. I didn't understand how he could act this way, how he could give up like this when there was a child's life at stake. Even though he didn't know her, he should at least care. He had children of his own.

"I am sorry, Emma," he said and put his phone back in his pocket. He handed me the file with all the work he had done over the past seven months. The work that I had paid him to do. "I did what I could, but it ends here."

I took the file from him with a snort. "Oh, it's not over on my end," I said and rose to my feet. I was speaking loudly now, and a few women sitting at a table next to us stopped their chatter and looked at me. "I am not done yet. I'll find another lawyer who can help me if you don't have the guts."

"Good luck with that, Emma," he said, leaning back in his chair. "No one will touch this case, and you know it because there is no case. You'll end up spending all your money on lawyers who won't be as honest with you as I am, and who'll get you nowhere. I am trying to save you the trouble and the money here. I'm being a friend."

I stopped at the door as he finished his sentence, then exhaled. I wanted to say something clever, but it just didn't come to me. I was too devastated. I pushed the door open and left the café, walking into the street, biting my lip not to cry, telling myself there were other ways to get Skye out of that place.

There simply had to be.

TWO

He was cold. So awfully cold, his teeth chattered, and his hands shook uncontrollably. If only he could get the heat back, get warmed up, but it was impossible. Being inside didn't help; sitting on the radiator until it almost burned him didn't help either. It was like this cold came from inside him and spread throughout his body, causing him to shiver and tremble, no matter how high he turned up the heat. And now it was disturbing his vision too; if he didn't know better, he'd swear his eyeballs were frozen and his brain covered in ice.

That's how it felt.

Lars staggered across the street downtown, then bumped into a woman holding her child by the hand. His shoulder knocked against hers as he tried to keep his balance, but the world kept moving beneath his feet, and the houses were swaying. The woman yelled at him and pushed him away as he tumbled into her.

"Hey! Look where you're going!"

The push made him stagger toward a streetlamp, and he reached his hands out to grab it, to hold on to it, but he missed it and fell forward, headfirst into the snow. He lay there, grunting at first, then sat up and felt the snow on his face, and removed a chunk that had stuck to his cheek. That's when he realized that the snow almost felt warm to the touch like he was colder than it was.

"What the heck?" he said and tossed the chunk by his feet. He rose in such a hurry that he lost his balance, then staggered toward a family of four walking on the sidewalk, holding hands. He tried to avoid them at all costs but lost his balance again and bumped right into a young child, tipping her over.

"What do you think you're doing, you idiot?" the father yelled.

"I'm so... so..."

Lars tried to help the crying girl back up when the father grabbed him by the collar and pulled him away.

"Get away from my daughter," he growled while the mom helped the girl get up, carrying her in her arms, giving him a look that could kill.

"I'm sorr..." he tried again to excuse himself. He wanted to explain himself, but the dad was in his face, his fist clenched.

His wife placed a hand on his shoulder to calm him down. "It's okay. Nothing happened," she said. "He's just some drunk."

The dad calmed down and collected himself, then shook his head. He grabbed his other child by the hand, then pulled him away from Lars, and they continued their walk. Lars rose to his feet, almost feeling like the snow was burning his skin; that's how wonderfully warm it felt.

"I gotta get out of here. I gotta get..." he mumbled when he slipped and fell again. A couple passing him shook their heads with a loud tsk-tsk, then moved on, while he struggled to get up once again, holding on to the streetlamp, pulling himself up.

He stood up against it for a few seconds, trying to regain his balance, looking down the street, where people's faces blended together with the buildings behind them, and the street swayed up and down. He closed his eyes briefly to make it stop, but as he opened them again, it was still there. And so was the cold—that infamous jarring cold. He couldn't stand it, this loathsome darn freezing sensation. It almost felt like his blood had frozen in his veins.

Lars looked at his arm and pulled his jacket up along with the sweater beneath it to look at his arm. It was turning purple at the wrist, almost black. Seeing this, Lars gasped and began to move forward once again, to get the blood flowing in his body. His right leg became stiff, and he could no longer bend it, so he dragged it behind him, then he felt his left arm stiffen as well and then his shoulder. He pulled off his glove with the other hand, and three of his fingers detached and stayed inside of it, while the two others were black as coal.

"What in the... help..." he gasped, then looked around, the wobbly world spinning fast. "Help! Help me!"

But people just walked past him, shaking their heads, the snow creaking beneath their boots. Lars stood still, unable to even move his eyes or turn his neck. His entire body became stiff as a stick, and just as a woman exited the door to a café next to him, he fell.

THREE

I had just closed the door to Café Mimosa behind me when something fell into my arms. At first, I was startled and let out a small shriek, but then I realized it was a person, a young man. He fell into my arms, and I grabbed him just as he was about to go down. His body felt as stiff as a board, and as I got myself gathered and realized I wasn't being attacked and robbed, I looked at his face in my arms. His eyes had rolled back, and he wasn't conscious. I tried to keep my balance while holding him, then let him slide slowly to the ground. I glared at his face, then tried to tap his cheeks to wake him.

"Sir, sir, are you there? Wake up; wake up."

The young man didn't react. That frightened me, and I yelled at random strangers walking past me.

"Help! Someone, please call for an ambulance."

The door behind me opened, and Michael came out. "Emma! What's going on?"

"This... this guy fell... just as I came out. He's not responding. Call for help, please."

Michael fumbled with his phone, and I heard him talk to the dispatcher. Meanwhile, I tried to wake the guy, but there was no life in him. He felt freezing cold to the touch, and his skin was turning black. These long branch-like stripes were moving up his throat and soon passed his chin and reached into his cheeks, painting him black.

"W-what are those?" I asked, my voice shaking.

Michael looked at it from behind me. "I... I don't know. I don't think I've ever seen anything like it."

"He's so cold," I said. "His skin. It almost hurts to touch him, like touching ice too long."

Michael shook his head. "Dr. Williamsen is on his way. So are the police and an ambulance."

He stared at the man's skin and then at his fingers. "He's missing three fingers. And look at the others. They're completely black. It almost looks like... frostbite."

Our eyes met, and my heart sank. It wasn't normal for people around here to get frostbite. We had snow, yes, and cold, but it wasn't that cold usually. Not enough to get frostbite like this. People who were homeless were known to occasionally get it if they slept outside and were drunk instead of going to the shelter, but never like this. This looked like he had been to the North Pole or tried to climb Mount Everest. Where had he gotten frostbitten like this? It was all over his body.

"We need to keep him warm until they get here. I'll get a blanket from inside the café," Michael said and walked back inside. Meanwhile, I leaned in over the stiff body.

"Hello? Can you hear me?"

His eyes opened briefly, and he looked at me. The look in them was intense. He grabbed my hand in his, and I felt the freezing cold spread through my body, and I shivered.

"I'm... so... cold," he whispered, then exhaled deeply and sank back into the snow.

I touched his cheek, but it felt almost like it stung me. That's how cold it was. I removed my hand, then felt for a pulse on his throat, putting my fingers on top of the blackened skin.

There wasn't any.

"No. No. No," I said, almost crying while I pressed my fingers hard onto the freezing cold skin, even though it hurt the tips of my fingers.

"Don't you die on me, not on my watch."

Michael returned and put a blanket on him. He wrapped his stiff body in it while I frantically searched for a pulse, but still didn't find any.

"Is he breathing?" Michael asked.

I leaned over him, then looked at his chest. It wasn't moving. I felt his throat again, then his wrist. Then I shook my head, tears springing to my eyes.

"I think... he's gone."

FOUR

The island's only ambulance arrived, driven by Dr. Williamsen's wife. Dr. Williamsen stepped out with his old brown medical bag in his hand, pushing back the thick glasses that kept sliding down his nose. He knelt next to the man and felt for a pulse, while I tried hard to stifle my tears. I didn't know this young man, but for some reason, he had chosen my arms to die in, and that made me so sad.

"Who is he?" Dr. Williamsen asked.

I shook my head. "I... we don't know. He just walked up the street and fell into my arms, and then he looked briefly at me and told me he was cold, and then he... he..."

Tears welled up in my eyes when Morten drove up in his police car and jumped out.

"Emma? Are you okay? What happened?"

He looked at the man in front of me. For a minute, I completely forgot we weren't together anymore, not since his nineteen-year-old daughter, Jytte, tried to kill herself, and he realized he had to focus on taking care of her, that he hadn't room for romance in his life as well. I threw myself into his arms. "Oh, Morten. It was awful."

He grabbed me and hesitated a second before putting his arms around me. "It'll be okay, Emma. Just tell me what happened. Who is the guy?"

I shook my head with a sniffle and let go of Morten, then wiped my nose on my sleeve like I always told my children not to do.

"I... I don't know. He sort of just came out of nowhere, and then he... fell... and I caught him, and then he told me he was so cold, and then he... he died. I don't even know who he is."

Morten approached the body and knelt next to it. "He looks familiar; what happened to his skin?"

I shook my head. Dr. Williamsen did the same. "It looks almost like... frostbite," he said.

I nodded.

"Now I know where I have seen him before," Morten exclaimed. "He's a friend of Jytte's. They had classes together at the high school. I have seen him in pictures."

I swallowed. That meant someone here on this island had just lost their son. It was getting a little too close for comfort.

"I'll take him in for an autopsy," Dr. Williamsen said with a deep sigh and a slight shake to his head. "I wish I knew how long he had been outside and where he has been. I have never seen frostbite all over the body like this."

Morten helped the Williamsens get the stiff body on a stretcher and put it in the back of the ambulance. They took off, and suddenly it was just the two of us; Michael had rushed back to his office. I just realized how awkward it was, and it made me even sadder.

Morten placed a hand on my shoulder. "Will you be okay, Emma? Do you need a ride home?"

I shook my head. I actually was dying for a ride because I had quite the walk home, but the last thing I wanted was to sit in his police car with him, nothing but an awkward silence between us.

"I'll be fine," I said.

"Are you sure? It looks like it'll snow again soon. There are some dark clouds approaching."

I nodded, knowing I would regret this as soon as I was striding my way through the snowstorm, but so be it. I hated being anywhere close to him these days since he was the one who had broken it off between us. I missed him so much it hurt, but I didn't want him to know that.

"I'll be fine, Morten. Just go. You have a report to write."

He gave me another look like he was trying to determine if I was being honest with him, then turned around and went back to his car. I watched him drive off, just as I felt the first snowflake fall on the tip of my nose.

FIVE

When I finally reached my house, I looked like a fluffy snowman. I brushed most of it off on my doorstep, then stomped my boots to get rid of the last part before I let myself inside my old house. The door creaked loudly as I opened it, and I felt the warmth of the inside hit my face. I slammed the door shut behind me, then shook violently as I took off my coat, boots, and beanie, trying to get the heat back.

I had barely made it inside when my phone rang. I considered not answering because I wasn't in any mood to talk to anyone, but then looked at the display and realized it was from Fishy Pines, where Victor went to school.

Oh, no, now what?

"Hello? Emma Frost."

It was HP, Victor's psychiatrist, and the leader of the place. He exhaled deeply.

"Emma, Victor ran away again."

I closed my eyes and rubbed my forehead. My fingers were still freezing, and I couldn't wait to get a warm cup of chocolate between them. Maybe with a couple of marshmallows in it. After the long walk, I sure deserved a little sugar.

"Again?" I said. "Why don't you keep an eye on him?"

With the phone clutched to my ear, I walked into the living room and looked out into the garden. As suspected, there I found Victor, sitting in the snow, looking up at the tree where he had found Skye.

"Don't put this on us, Emma. You know we can't stop him once he decides to go. He did it again today when they had outside time; he somehow blasted the gate open and ran. No one dares to get close to him when he does those things."

"I guess not," I said.

"I'll have to have a chat with him about his behavior when he comes back tomorrow," he said. "We won't tolerate this."

That made me laugh. "Good luck with that."

"It's not funny, Emma. We're trying our best with him. If he doesn't get better, then I see no other way out than admitting him full-time to the psych ward. He can't run away from there."

My heart dropped. "Oh, no, HP anything but that. He won't be able to take it being away from home."

"There are medications we can give him that'll keep him calm," he continued unabated. "By not helping us out, you're contributing to his continuing lack of education. That is not good, Emma. He needs to go to school. It's the law. And he needs treatment. If you're refusing him that, then I see no other way out than to admit him."

That wiped the grin straight off my face. Was he seriously threatening to take my boy? Nothing seemed scarier to me right at this moment.

"He'll be back tomorrow," I said. "And he'll stay this time. I'll make sure he does. Don't worry."

"I'm glad to hear that," HP said, sounding so smug I wanted to scream. He hung up.

I stared at the phone, then at my son outside the big windows. Daniel snuck up behind me without me hearing him. He startled me when he suddenly started to speak.

"It's weird; he won't go to school, and that is all I want. I am so bored here at the house."

I grabbed the boy's hand in mine, relieved to find it solid. It was wet like he had just washed it, but that's how his skin was these days. He was becoming more and more like his mother, and soon he'd probably be rushing through the sewers like she was. That was why we needed to keep him hidden.

If the people at Omicon knew he had developed these powers, they'd go out of their way to take him back. And I promised Lyn to protect him from them. I hadn't seen her since she left her son with me, and I just prayed she was still alive, that the goons from Omicon hadn't taken her back to the place she and Skye escaped from together. They had found Skye, but I felt confident that Lyn was still out there.

"I know, sweetie," I said. "I'm sure Victor would love to switch places with you anytime. He hates it there. But that's how it is right now, and it has to stay that way. Let me make us all some afternoon hot chocolate. Then we can read a little, huh? You can read to me. Would you like that?"

I had been teaching Daniel how to read and do maths because he didn't go to school. I couldn't contribute much to maths because that wasn't my strong suit at all, but my daughter, Maya, had helped him out too, and she was very good at it. She was still dating his older brother, Alexander, and they were very happy together, even though he didn't know Daniel lived here with us.

Daniel wasn't his biological brother, as his family had adopted him. Their dad worked for Omicon and would do anything to get him back if he knew Daniel was here, so he could use him for their experiments as well, just like they were doing right now to Skye.

Skye. Just saying her name made me feel sick with guilt. How hadn't I been able to take better care of her? I knew those people would come for her; I knew they wanted her. They came here and threatened me, yet I sent them away, thinking we were safe in our house, that Skye was safe with me. How could I have been so stupid? The poor girl was in my care. She put her trust in me. Why hadn't I moved her somewhere else? Why hadn't I sent her to the mainland to stay at a friend's house somewhere? Or just taken her to my friend Sophia's house across the street where they wouldn't know to look? Why hadn't I protected her?

I sighed and looked at my son outside. The snow was still falling heavily, and his snowsuit and beanie had turned white. I wondered if he was cold, but Victor usually never felt the cold much, or heat for that matter.

That's why. Victor is why you didn't move her.

I exhaled, thinking I had just been selfish. I knew it would have killed Victor if they couldn't be together all the time. Just like it was killing him now to have to miss her this terribly. And it was killing me that I was the only one who could do anything about it, the only one who cared enough to.

I just wasn't doing enough.

SIX

"I don't understand where you went."

Nina looked at Ingrid. They were sitting in Ingrid's room, on the floor, while the freezing wind howled outside the window. It had gotten dark as it usually did about five o'clock at this time of year, and they could see the snowflakes dancing in the light from the streetlamps.

Ingrid swallowed her warm hot chocolate. Her mom had made drinks for them both when Nina came to visit. It felt good as it slid down her throat, warming her up from the inside. Yet she still felt cold and wrapped herself in a blanket.

"You were just gone," Nina continued. "Why did you leave?"

Ingrid's eyes avoided hers. "I... I don't really know. That's the odd part. I remember us being in the clearing and Tanja dancing and raising the cup, and then I don't remember anything else."

Nina wrinkled her nose. It was obvious to Ingrid that she didn't believe her. Her parents had shared that same look on their faces when she told them what had happened—the little she remembered.

"But... but where did you go? We looked everywhere for you," Nina continued. "We went through the entire park, then called the police and your parents and everything. They searched all night for you. And then you show up the next morning on the beach."

Ingrid sighed. She shook her head. "I don't know. I woke up in the snow in the dunes. I have no recollection of going there or even leaving you. They thought I might have had an aneurysm, but the doctors said I was perfectly normal. Their scans didn't find anything abnormal. My parents are convinced I had been drinking or smoking marijuana."

Nina cleared her throat. "It wouldn't be the first time. But... did you?"

Ingrid shook her head. "No. But no one believes me."

Nina scoffed. "You have to admit it's kind of hard to believe you weren't high or something."

"But I wasn't," Ingrid said, annoyed.

It was so irritating that people kept asking her about this, not wanting to believe anything she told them. The fact was, she had disappeared and been gone for an entire night without knowing where she had been. It was scary to think about. She could have been raped and not know it. Yet somehow, she knew that hadn't happened.

It was something else, something that had to do with the two swollen red dots on her shoulder. Mosquito bites, the doctor had said when she asked about them. But what kind of mosquitos were alive at this time of year? Sure, if it had been summer, she would have bought into that explanation, but not at this time of year. Plus, they didn't look like any mosquito bites that Ingrid had ever had before.

"I might as well let you know right away because you'll figure this out soon enough," Nina said, "but Tanja has told us to stay away from you, and you're out of the coven. She believes you did this on purpose to mock us all. You never took the coven seriously, she said, and weren't into it. She's found another girl to take your spot. I just thought you should know. That's why I came by. I guess I felt like I owed it to you."

Nina rose to her feet and grabbed her jacket, then put it on. She sent Ingrid half a smile, then shrugged.

"I kind of liked you, so I'm a little sad about this, but I don't really have a choice. I don't want to get on Tanja's bad side."

Ingrid smiled halfheartedly. "I get it."

Nina left with a shrug, and Ingrid sat on the floor of her room, where she heard the front door slam shut.

Her mom peeked in. "You okay in here?"

Sure. I'm great! I no longer have a friend in the world, and no one believes me when I say something happened to me, something awful, but hey, I'm great!

Ingrid forced a smile to calm her mother. She had been so worried since Ingrid was found on the beach a week ago. She didn't want her to be concerned. She didn't want her to know that Ingrid was terrified to the bone of what had happened because she didn't remember anything, or that she felt lonelier than ever.

"I'll be fine," she said.

Her mother's eyes grew dark. It was obvious she didn't believe her.

"Okay. Good. You know, your dad and I are here for you if you need us, okay? If you want to talk."

Ingrid nodded reassuringly. "I'll be fine, Mom. Promise."

SEVEN

"I'm sorry to ask to hang out at your place, but my house right now is just an awful place to be."

Alexander looked at Maya across the kitchen. They had walked back to her house after meeting up downtown. They had both graduated high school a few months earlier. She had started working at a local gas station downtown, while he spent all day at home because his father wanted him to go to med school, but Alex wasn't sure that's what he wanted. He used his mother's death last year as an excuse for wanting some time off.

Both his parents were doctors and had always thought that's what their son was going to be as well. But the past few months before graduation, he had started doubting if that was what he wanted. He had told Maya he'd rather just stay on the island and hang out with her while figuring out what he wanted to do with his life... if he wanted to pursue medicine or not. Right now, he just knew he didn't want to go to school anymore.

Maya felt the same way; she needed a break from it all, but her mother had told her she needed something to do. If she didn't go to school, she'd better get a job. She needed a reason to get up in the morning. Now, she was saving up for a trip to

South America in the spring. Backpacking for three months with her best friend, Christina. She had started planning and felt very good about their plans. She'd apply for university next year. She was in no rush.

"I know, sweetie," she said and pulled the teabag out of his cup, then handed it to him. She sat down and sipped her own tea while thinking about Daniel, hoping he was in his room upstairs. She had texted her mom and told her they were coming home, so she assumed she had made sure the boy was nowhere in sight. Maya hated keeping this secret from Alexander: that they were harboring his little brother while his father was still searching for him everywhere.

"How's your dad coping?" she asked.

"Actually, a lot better than I'd expect," he said. "He doesn't talk about Daniel at all when I'm around. But I overheard him talking on the phone about this team they have out searching for him. It's all a little odd if you ask me. He's behaving strangely, and I can't stand it. That's why I didn't want to hang out at my house. I can't stand being there. It's like he's keeping a ton of secrets from me, always lowering his voice when having people over or talking on the phone when I enter the room. It's annoying. I can't wait to get out of there. I am just not sure med school is the right thing for me."

"But didn't you get accepted?" Maya said. "Why don't you just give it a try?"

He leaned over and grabbed her hand in his. "It'll be there next year as well. I can't stand the thought of going to school now. And especially not being away from you. I would only be able to see you on the weekends, and right now, I couldn't bear that."

Maya smiled. She felt the same. She had wanted to take this trip with Christina for a very long time but was beginning to feel the doubt nag inside her. But the thing was, she had once made a promise to herself that she wouldn't stay home from a trip like that for some boy. Plus, she had promised Christina they'd go. She couldn't let her down because of a boy. It was, after all, only for three months. It would do.

"Well, hello there, Alex," Maya's mom said as she entered the kitchen. "How are you doing? How are things at home? How's your dad coping? Any news about Daniel?"

Maya gave her mother a stern look.

Way too many questions, Mom. Can't you hear how suspicious that sounds?

Maya's mom was the worst at keeping secrets or lying, especially to people she cared about. Maya was terrified that Alex would find out she had been keeping this huge secret from him these past seven months while they had been dating. It was the worst thing she had ever done to anyone, and she often fought with her mother about it because she wanted to tell him. But she couldn't, her mother said. They had promised to keep the boy safe, and that's what they'd do.

"He's surviving," Alex said with a smile. "And so am I."

Alex was very fond of Maya's mom and thought her being a famous author was so cool. "But it's tough. Daniel has been gone for seven months now, and hope is diminishing, you know? With my mom gone as well, the house is very empty."

Maya's mom nodded. It was so obvious she was trying to suppress a nervous smile. Maya hoped she'd just leave.

He's gonna dump me the day he finds out. He's gonna hate me for the rest of his life, and it's all her fault.

"Let us know if there is anything we can do to help," she said. "It must be awful for you, not knowing where he is or what happened to him."

Maya's mom said the last part while her glance slid toward the stairs, and Maya felt certain that Alex noticed.

Please, just leave, Mom. Please. Before you reveal everything. You're so obvious. Can't you see it?

"Hello? Is anyone home?"

A face peeked inside the kitchen. It was Sophia, her mother's friend and neighbor. Sophia lived across the street with her six children. She knew everything that took place at Maya's house.

Great. One more to act suspicious.

"Ah, hello, Maya... and Alex." Sophia's smile froze, and she glared at Maya's mother, her eyes wide like her mind was screaming, *What's he doing here? What if he finds out?*

Knowing that Sophia was as bad a liar and as bad at keeping a secret hidden as her mom, if not worse, Maya rose to her feet, the chair screeching as it was pushed back across the floor. She had to get Alex out of here before either of them said something that would reveal everything and destroy her life.

"Maybe we should go to my room," she said and grabbed Alex's hand in hers. "So, we can be alone for a little while."

She pulled his arm almost forcefully, and he had to put down his cup.

"Come, Alex. Let's go. Now."

EIGHT

Alexander stayed for dinner, so I had to serve Daniel his food in his room. He didn't mind much, even though it was hard to explain to him why he couldn't eat with his own brother or even see him. I knew Alex was a good boy, and maybe he wouldn't tell his dad where Daniel was if we told him why he couldn't, but I didn't want to risk it. I wasn't sure I wanted more kids involved. It wasn't an easy thing to understand, and it would mean risking that Alex might think I was a nutcase and maybe even had kidnapped his brother.

Sophia left right before we sat down. She helped me peel the potatoes, and we had a glass of wine while talking about what had happened downtown. I told her about the guy who had fallen into my arms and then died. She had already heard everything about it from some other neighbor but wanted to hear the story from me as well.

"His name was Lars Madsen," she told me. "Karin Madsen's son, you know the one who works at the travel agency downtown, the one with the high-pitched voice."

"Oh, yeah, I know her. I didn't know she had a son."

"Well, he was twenty, so a little older than Maya. He was

known to be some party animal lately. The dad left the island many years ago, while Lars was still in high school. It messed the boy up, they say. He adored his father, and the mom lost control of him while she wallowed in sadness over the divorce. Lars started partying and drinking and only barely graduated. You could always find him at the local bars downtown. He was known to stay until they closed in the early morning hours. They say he was drunk when he died, that he staggered through downtown before he ran into you."

I sipped my wine, then put the glass down while shaking my head. I thought for a brief second about my parents, who were traveling through Italy and would be gone for about a month. I missed them, especially my dad. He was so easy to talk to.

"I don't think he was drunk."

"Then on drugs," Sophia said.

I exhaled pensively.

"You don't think he was on drugs either?" she asked.

"This was something completely different. He was so cold to the touch, and he had frostbite. He had lost three of his fingers too. They were still inside his glove."

Sophia made a face. "Yuk. Could he have been drunk and then slept in the snow?"

I shook my head. "I don't know. I hardly think it's cold enough for that around here, do you?"

Sophia hadn't been able to answer and had left me hanging on that question when her oldest daughter texted her that the kids were hungry.

I finished making the dinner and ate with Maya, Alex, and Victor, hoping that Victor didn't suddenly say something about Daniel to reveal his whereabouts to Alex, but he didn't. Victor knew how to keep a secret and wanted to help his friend. The last thing Daniel needed was to go back to that house and his so-called father.

After dinner, Alex was picked up by his dad, Christopher Finnerup. He came to the door and rang the doorbell. I felt sweat tickle my forehead as I went to open the door. His eyes were icy and stern as they fell on me. It made me nervous.

"Hello, Dr. Finnerup," I said and tilted my head, pretending to show sympathy. "How are you holding up?"

Christopher Finnerup snorted lightly, then sighed. It came off as fake and very forced. "It's not easy. I can tell you that much. Imagine if Victor went missing and was nowhere to be found. I just want my son back."

So you can take him back to that lab and do your little experiments on him, back to the place where no one hears you scream.

"I bet it is tough," I said, biting back my feelings of disgust for this man. "Let me know if there is anything we can do to help."

"I don't think there is much you can do unless you're hiding him in your house, heh," he said with a vague grin.

My eyes grew wide, and I could barely swallow as the words fell.

"I'm sorry," he said and placed a hand on my shoulder. "I was just trying to make a joke. It wasn't very funny, I guess. Is Alex ready?"

NINE

The next morning, Victor seemed more distant than usual over breakfast. He was staring into his cereal bowl and hadn't looked up once.

"What's with you, buddy?" I asked and sipped my coffee. "You barely touched your food."

He didn't answer but kept looking into the cereal.

"You gotta eat something, Victor. Or else you'll be hungry later. You know the teachers don't allow you to snack. You can't go till lunch on an empty stomach. You'll get grumpy, and we can't have that."

Still, there was no response from my son. I was used to him not answering if the conversation was boring or just not interesting enough. His lack of social skills was part of why he needed to go to Fishy Pines, where he received a combined treatment by psychiatrists and education by teachers trained to handle someone like him with special needs. But somehow, this silence seemed different from usual.

I sighed and put my cup down. I crossed my arms in front of my chest and studied my son.

"You still haven't told me why you ran away yesterday. Did something happen at school?"

No reaction. Not even movement. He just sat there with his curly hair hanging down in front of his face, covering his eyes. I had tried so many times yesterday to get him to explain this to me, why he ran away again. I figured it was just because of Skye, but now I was worried that it could be something else. Something he had a hard time telling me about for some reason.

"Victor, dang it. If you want me to help you, you need to start talking to me. Is it just because you miss Skye? Or is something else going on? Are the kids there teasing you? Are the teachers not being nice to you? Is it HP? What is it? Please, say something,"

I rubbed my forehead and sighed. When he still didn't answer, I rose to my feet and began cleaning up.

"The bus will be here shortly. You should get ready."

Another silence followed, then Victor said something that I couldn't make out because he was speaking so low. I turned to look at him. "What did you say?"

"I don't want to go," he said, suddenly speaking up.

I pulled my chair up close to him and sat down. "And why is that? Could you please explain a little further?"

"No."

"What do you mean, no? If you're not going to tell me more, then you're going on the bus when it gets here in ten minutes."

"No," he said again.

"You can't just say no, Victor."

"Why not?"

I threw out my arms. "Because... I need an explanation. At least something I can tell the school. They called here yesterday and threatened me. If you don't go to school today, they said you'd be in trouble—or rather, I would. Do you understand what this means? It means you have to go, Victor. I can't let you stay here."

"Why not?"

"Because I say so, okay? That's how the world works. You can't just not go because you don't feel like it. Just like people can't not go to work. There are certain things in life you have to do. You can't just not do them because you don't feel like it."

"Why not? I said I don't want to."

"Not good enough, buddy," I said. "I'm sorry. You gotta learn this at some point. This is life, Victor, doing what you're supposed to do. Most kids would never go to school if their parents let them stay at home just because they didn't feel like going. You need an education, Victor. That's just the way it is. You might as well accept it."

I rose to my feet and put the chair back at the table, then grabbed his cereal bowl and turned away from him to face the sink.

"But I'm cold," he said.

I almost dropped the bowl in the sink. I looked at him again, wrinkling my forehead.

"You're cold. What do you mean you're cold?"

I stared at my son, hardly blinking.

"Oh, my God, Victor, you're shivering."

I rushed to him and put a hand on his forehead. He wasn't warm. On the contrary, he felt freezing to the touch. It scared me deeply after what I had experienced the day before with Lars Madsen. Could there be some disease going around?

A disease where he gets freezing cold and frostbitten? Hardly, Emma. That's just silly. Victor was probably just out in the garden for too long this morning while I prepared breakfast. He got cold, and now he's using it to get to stay home. That's all.

Victor pulled away. He never liked it when I touched him. I pondered it for a few seconds, wondering what to do. On one side, I was certain Victor was just playing me, so he didn't have to go to school; on the other, I was scared he was actually getting sick. If it hadn't been for my encounter with that Lars fellow, then it would have been an easy decision, but something told me I needed to play it safe here. HP would have to understand it if the boy was sick, right? It could hardly be my fault if he came down with something. He couldn't punish us for that. Could he?

I exhaled. It didn't matter. I had to go with my gut here. And it told me something was off with Victor.

"Okay, that does it. You're staying home today, and I'll have Dr. Williamsen come to have a look at you. But there is no going into the garden and getting cold, do you hear me?"

Victor didn't answer. He rose to his feet, then left, rushing up the stairs to his room.

As I grabbed his chair to put it back in its place, it felt cold and touching it caused me to shiver.

TEN

"Victor didn't come in this morning. Again. I thought we had an agreement."

Less than half an hour after Victor was supposed to be at the school, HP called. He didn't sound angry. More like he was deeply annoyed with me, which he probably was.

"Remember our talk yesterday, Miss Frost?"

Suddenly, I was Miss Frost. Up until now, he had called me Emma. HP wasn't the type to be formal. He had to be really upset with me.

"I sure do," I said. "How could I forget? You basically threatened to take my son from me and admit him full-time."

"Then forgive me, but I don't understand why he is once again skipping school?"

"He is sick," I said. "A kid can get sick, right? I mean, it is allowed even at your school to get sick, right?"

HP sighed. I knew he was by now closing his eyes and rubbing his face as I had often seen him do when he tried to keep his composure around me. I didn't care. He could get as mad as he wanted. I wasn't going to send my son to school today, no matter what he said.

"And are you certain he is sick?"

"Of course," I said, trying my best to sound convincing. I wasn't succeeding very well. I was certain he could tell by the sound of my voice that I had my doubts. I knew that Victor was probably just trying to get out of going to school, and I guess I kind of let him. I was beginning to think I should find another school for him, but then we'd have to move away from the island, and I really didn't want that. I loved living here.

"I am going to need a little more than that," HP said. "I'm gonna have to ask for a doctor's note."

"I'll make sure you get that," I said. "As a matter of fact, Dr. Williamsen is on his way over. I just got off the phone with him."

HP went silent. I smiled triumphantly, knowing he hadn't expected that response.

"Well, okay then. Let me know what the doctor says," HP said.

We hung up, and I sighed, relieved. I was terrified after what he had said yesterday about admitting Victor and probably medicating him. To me, that was the worst scenario, the one I had feared since I realized my son wasn't like most children. I had fought to give him a childhood as normal as possible.

I walked upstairs to get dressed before the doctor arrived, then peeked into Maya's room. She had left early for her shift at the gas station. She planned to travel in the spring with her friend, and she was earning money for that trip. I felt awful that she was about to leave me. I knew she would be back after a few months away, but by then, she'd be ready to leave the nest and would start looking for a flat, probably in Copenhagen, hours from here.

She'd have to go away in order to get into a good college in the capital, and that was the end of it. I knew I should be proud, and of course, I was. She had grown up to be such an independent, beautiful, and strong woman, but I couldn't bear the thought of losing her to the world. I didn't want to share her.

I smiled secretively, then closed the door before I walked to Victor's room and peeked inside. Daniel was with him, and they were playing a computer game. I stared at my son, feeling my heart beat faster. I wouldn't be able to bear it if they took him away from me.

Barely had I finished the thought and closed the door, half choked up by my own angst-gripped thoughts when the doorbell rang downstairs. I rushed to my bedroom and threw on some clothes, then ran down the stairs and let in the doctor.

ELEVEN

Maya yawned and leaned on the counter in front of her. She had taken the early shift and had to get in before six o'clock this morning. She had trouble falling asleep the night before, and that was catching up to her now. The gas station was empty except for a young girl who was standing by the sweets.

"The poor girl," Angela, Maya's coworker, said, coming up behind her. She had just put on a new batch of hot dogs that stank up the whole place. Maya didn't know that anyone ate hot dogs this early in the morning until she started working at the gas station and watched the lorry drivers come in and ask for them along with the occasional drunk who had been awake all night.

Angela nodded toward the girl who had moved on to the bags of chips now. She picked one up and looked at it, then changed her mind and put it back on the shelf.

"Why do you say that?" Maya asked.

Angela's eyes grew wide. "You didn't hear?"

It was by far the sentence that excited Angela's lips the most. She was a twenty-five-year-old woman who never got away from the island after high school and now functioned as the island's center for gossip. Angela knew everything about everyone on the island. In so many ways, Angela's story served as an example of how Maya definitely didn't want to end up. Looking at her and listening to her pushed Maya to want to travel, to want to go away for college. If this was how young people ended up if they stayed, then she had no choice. She had to get out of there.

"I can't say I have," Maya answered.

Maya could see the thrill written on Angela's face. There was nothing better to her than someone who *hadn't heard.*

She lowered her voice and stood to the side with Maya while she spoke, watching the girl's every move.

"Well, according to what I heard, she disappeared last Friday night while she and her friends were doing some sort of Wiccan ritual at the park. She didn't turn up till the next morning, and, get this, according to her own story, she woke up on the beach, naked."

Maya wrinkled her forehead. "And where had she been?"

"That's the beauty of it. She says she doesn't know. Can you believe that? I sure can't. I mean, of course, she remembers. Probably ran off with some dude and then regretted having sex with him in the dunes. Or maybe she was so drunk she just blacked out. Maybe she just fell asleep on the beach."

"But... if she was naked, she can't have been on the beach all night," Maya said. "It would have been freezing."

Angela nodded. "You have a point."

"Where were her clothes found?"

"Well, apparently they had all gotten naked, you know for the ritual, the witch or Wiccan or pagan or whatever they call it. So, the other girls had her clothes with them. But they say that she just suddenly vanished. I think she must have been drunk already, then ran off, maybe met some guy who took advantage of her, took her home with him before he threw her out the next morning, and she staggered down to the beach. That's what I think. But look at her. Poor bastard must know how the entire island is talking about her. Well, her and that Lars guy who died on the street yesterday, drunk out of his mind."

Maya stared at Angela. She wanted to tell her that the guy died in her mother's arms and that he wasn't drunk at all, but for some reason, she didn't. She didn't want to start new rumors or make his death any more spectacular than it already was to people like Angela.

The girl had moved on to the magazines and was flipping through one when she seemed to notice they were talking about her and put the magazine back. She sent Maya a look, then suddenly hurried out of the shop, leaving the magazine on the wrong shelf.

"I'll get it," Maya said, then walked out on the other side of the counter. She grabbed the magazine in her hands, then realized it was covered in white frost.

TWELVE

She was supposed to be in school, but she didn't go. Ingrid had left her house with the intention of going, but then changed her mind and rode her bike to the gas station instead. She didn't know why she didn't want to go. Probably because she was terrified of going, of facing Tanja again, and of spending a day with no friends.

She knew how they were talking about her behind her back. She had seen it all week long and heard the whispering that died out as soon as she approached them. She had seen the looks and the noses that were lifted toward the sky, and she knew what they thought. They believed she was a drunk and a slut.

So, she had thought she'd buy some sweets and maybe a magazine and go back home when she knew her parents had left for work and spend the day in bed instead, staying under the covers and trying to keep warm. But now it was all ruined. Those stupid girls at the gas station had been gossiping about her behind her back. She could tell by the looks on their faces and knew then that they were no different from the people at her school.

Ingrid stepped on the pedals and rushed her bike down the sidewalk. Most people had been out early shoveling the snow in front of their houses, but a few hadn't, so she had to get off and push the bike through the thick snow. Her hands and arms were freezing, and it was like she couldn't get the warmth back. The cold hurt her bones, and she was constantly shivering.

Ingrid reached her house, then parked the bike in the garage and went inside, using the back door. She had seen her mom's car in the garage and knew her parents hadn't left for work yet. They usually drove downtown together as they worked at the same accounting company. Her mom was actually her dad's supervisor, which caused some friction in their marriage from time to time.

As she went through the kitchen, she could hear them speaking in low voices in the living room. Hearing her name mentioned, she stopped and listened by the door.

"I don't know what to do, Jacob," her mom said. "She's not herself. Something is wrong. Ever since she was found on that... beach, something has been off with her."

"She's fine," her dad said. "I'm sure it's just the shock. She won't be drinking again or smoking anything; that's for sure. Maybe it can serve as a lesson."

"But that's what worries me. You heard the doctor at the hospital. She wasn't drunk or high. They didn't find anything in her bloodwork."

"Come on, Margaret. Of course, she was. How else do you explain the blackout? It's either that or she won't tell us what happened to her. Maybe she doesn't want us to know what really happened. I say we leave it alone. It's in all of our best interest."

Her mother sighed. "I don't know. I am so scared something is wrong with her. What if she has mental health issues? That can cause blackouts too."

"You think she has a mental illness?" he asked with a mocking laugh.

Her mother exhaled deeply. "I don't know. I just know something is wrong with her. She's constantly freezing, and her lips have that bluish color, have you noticed? I think she needs to see someone. I don't know if it's mental or physical or what. Something is not right, and I don't want to risk anything like this happening to her again. Why was she out on her own all night, naked? Why was she naked, Jacob?"

Her dad sighed now too. "I don't know, Margaret. How about we take her to see a psychiatrist? Maybe they can figure out what is going on with her. We're late for work. Can we talk about it in the car?"

Ingrid pulled away and rushed up the stairs to hide in her room. She sat by the door, panting agitatedly as she heard her parents leave downstairs, slamming the front door.

They think I'm crazy. Am I nuts?

She looked down at her hands that were purple. She reached over and touched the side of the dresser next to her and watched as the area she had touched turned to ice. Then she gasped and pulled her hand away.

"Maybe I am going crazy," she mumbled, staring at the frozen spot on the wood. "Maybe I am stark raving mad."

THIRTEEN

"He says he's freezing," I said when Dr. Williamsen had looked at Victor. We walked downstairs together, him carrying his brown bag. "And he's constantly shivering, so I thought he might have a fever."

Williamsen nodded, and we went into the kitchen, where I served him a cup of coffee.

"It is quite cold in your house, Emma," he said, warming his hands on the cup. "Maybe you should turn the heat up a little."

"I'll do that," I said and sipped my own coffee, then sat down. It was customary and expected that you'd serve the doctor coffee when he made house calls. I preferred to have him come to our house due to Victor's trouble being out in the world with people, and he had agreed that it was best for the boy.

"I don't see that anything should be wrong with the boy, though," he said, and I served him biscuits from a batch I had just pulled out of the cooker. He smiled and grabbed one. "He seems fine; he doesn't have a fever... but..."

A small furrow grew between the doctor's eyes like he was pondering something.

"But what?" I asked, slightly nervous. "Is something else wrong?"

He sipped his coffee. "I don't think so. But... well, his temperature, as I said it didn't show a fever, on the contrary."

"What? Was it too low?" I said, meant as a joke.

"Yes, exactly. It was a little low."

"How little?" I asked, a biscuit halfway down my throat.

"Well, normal body temperature is thirty-seven degrees Celsius, you know that, but he was about thirty-five degrees. Does he usually have a low body temperature? Some people run a little lower than others."

I shook my head. "No. Usually, he's the normal temperature when he's not sick. Is that a problem?"

The doctor shook his head. "I can't see why it would be. Just as I couldn't find anything wrong with him, except him being very cold to the touch and having a low body temperature."

I smiled anxiously, thinking about Lars Madsen and how cold he had felt to the touch. I swallowed.

"But he isn't sick."

"I wouldn't assume so, no. But keep an eye on it and try to turn up the heat in this house. That'll probably do the trick."

He smiled in a way that let me know he too was puzzled by this discovery, and I didn't know what to say. We sat in silence for a little, eating biscuits, and the doctor had several more.

"These are really good," he said with crumbs on his lips.

"So, it's not like there's some disease going around where people freeze or something, right?"

He laughed. "Heavens, no. I haven't heard of such a disease."

Again, silence between us.

"You're thinking about Lars Madsen, aren't you?"

"How can I not?" I asked. "He died in my arms."

Dr. Williamsen looked into his coffee. He was so obviously avoiding my eyes. He'd forgotten how well I knew him.

"What did he die from anyway?" I asked, sensing there was something the man wasn't telling me. "Did you do the autopsy?"

His eyes lifted and met mine.

"You did. And what did you find out?"

FOURTEEN

"His heart stopped due to hypothermia," Dr. Williamsen said. "His body temperature was zero degrees Celsius. I took it when he was found, you know, to determine the time of death because the body loses about one-point-five degrees per hour. Normally, it would have been about thirty-three. Sometimes a little lower if he's been dead long, but never that low. And this guy hadn't been dead long. He was very much alive when he bumped into you."

I almost spat out my coffee while the doctor spoke. "So, his body temperature was below freezing?"

Dr. Williamsen nodded, still pensively. "And there was something else that I have never seen before. His blood was frozen in his veins. All his organs were frozen solid."

I made a face. "Yuk. How is that possible?"

He shrugged while I grabbed another biscuit. It was still warm as it landed on my tongue and the chocolate melted in my mouth. "What could have caused something like that?"

Dr. Williamsen shook his head. "I have never seen anything like it. I mean, old Leonard froze to death on the harbor many years ago. He had fallen asleep on one of our toughest winter nights ever recorded back in the nineties. But he didn't even look like Lars when I did his autopsy to make sure no crime had been committed. Some conditions might cause a low body temperature, even if a patient hasn't been out in the cold. It may be caused by alcohol or drug use, going into shock, or certain disorders like diabetes or low thyroid. Low body temperature may also occur with an infection, but that is most common in newborns, older adults, or frail people. But it doesn't cause this severe degree of hypothermia. If I didn't know better, I'd say his blood froze while he was still alive, and that caused his heart to stop, but that isn't possible."

"So, he didn't freeze to death after being outside all night, is that what you're saying?"

"It would require temperatures outside that were lower than zero degrees Celsius. We don't have temperatures like that around here. Yes, we have frost and snow, but we usually stay about freezing. And how was he still conscious? Usually, when a body reaches a temperature of thirty-five, the shivering, weakness, and confusion set in. At twenty-seven degrees, a person will lose consciousness. At twenty-one, the hypothermia is profound, and death can occur. This guy was at zero. Yes, he was dead at the time but hadn't been for more than an hour. That means his body temperature was about zero degrees when he fell into your arms.

"The cold temperature would have hindered the heart and the brain from functioning properly for a long time before that. The improper functioning of the heart would have resulted in reduced blood flow to many organs, putting the body in a state of shock. He'd have kidney failure and liver failure long before he made it into the street. How was he able to still walk up to you? I don't get it. I have never seen anything like it. The most damage was done inside him. Usually, it's the fingers and the skin that get frostbitten first, but he didn't have that. Inside him was a different story. His organs were completely black and frozen solid. It was almost like he froze from the inside out."

Dr. Williamsen finished his coffee and sent me a vague smile.

"Listen to me babbling on." He rose to his feet and grabbed his brown bag. He pushed his glasses back, then sent me a look.

"I'm gonna have his body sent to the mainland and have them take a look at him in Copenhagen as well. They might come up with an explanation because I sure can't. Thank you for the coffee and biscuits. You don't mind if I grab one for the road, do you?"

"If you write me a doctor's note for Victor's school, then you can take all of them," I said with a wink.

FIFTEEN

"We need something spectacular, something that will make people remember you."

Lisa Rasmussen looked up at Camilla, her campaign manager. They were sitting in her office at city hall, on the yellow couches Lisa had brought in even though there was barely room for them. She wanted it to be like the US president's Oval Office in the White House that she had always admired in films.

Everyone told her she was crazy, that there wasn't room for an arrangement like this, but she made it happen anyway. And then she fired those who had told her she couldn't do it. She wanted to surround herself with people who believed in the impossible. The rest had nothing to do in her city hall.

Yes, it was her city hall. As soon as she had become mayor of Fanoe island, it had become hers, and she made sure everyone knew it. If they didn't support her, or if they criticized her choices, they were out. It was as easy as that.

Lisa nodded pensively when listening to Camilla's statistics. A new election was coming up this month, and she wasn't looking too good in the polls. Her approval rating was lower than any mayor before her, Camilla said. But it didn't scare Lisa. What Camilla didn't know was that Lisa had something up her sleeve, something that would once again put her up on top and make the people of Fanoe island want to reelect her. Heck, they might even agree to put up that statue of her that she tried to get them to about a year ago but was voted down.

They're gonna beg me to stay on as their mayor. They're gonna praise me and want to remember me forever. I helped put Fanoe island on the map. When things looked the worst in ages, I turned it all around. They'll be eternally grateful for that and not only put up a statue but also name a street or a square after me. Of course, they will.

Thinking of this, already hearing the cheers, Lisa grinned while Camilla continued to show her graphs and statistics. She stopped.

"What?" Camilla asked.

Lisa shook her head. "Oh, nothing."

"If you have something that will help us in this campaign, then please tell me. It would be so great. I am seriously out of ideas."

Lisa sat up straight and leaned forward. "I have something."

Camilla's eyes grew wide, and a smile of relief spread across her face.

"Really? That's wonderful. We really need something right now, something big. What is it?"

"I can't tell you. At least not yet."

Camilla exhaled and sank back on the couch. "How am I supposed to use it if you can't even tell me?"

"I will tell you," Lisa said, and sipped her coffee with oat milk. "In due time."

"And when is that? There are only three weeks until the election. We've got to move fast. Can't you at least give me a hint?"

Lisa leaned back, a smug look on her face. "All right. I can't go into detail, but I want you to arrange a press conference later today. I can reveal a little for the press, just enough to raise curiosity. Tease them slightly. How about that?"

Camilla sighed, satisfied. "That would be awesome. Let me get on it right away."

SIXTEEN

"What? No biscuits? I thought I smelled freshly baked ones all the way across the street."

Sophia walked into my kitchen and sat down. Her youngest daughter Alma looked up at me with big blue eyes.

"No biscuits?"

"I am sorry, sweetie," I said with a soft smile. That girl was so adorable with her soft curls surrounding her face that I could hardly stand it. "The doctor was here, and he ate a lot because he was very hungry, and he even took the rest of them with him home to his wife. So, I'm afraid I don't have any more left."

Alma made a groaning sound, then hurried to the living room where I had kept some of Victor's old toys for her to play with. We needed the little one distracted while we talked.

I poured coffee for Sophia, and she held the cup between her hands. "Ah, I needed that."

I sat down. "What's up? Everything okay at home?"

That made Sophia laugh out loud. "With six children, nothing is ever okay. Especially not teenagers. I can't get a word out of Christoffer these days. Kind of makes me miss those days when he was younger, even though he drove me nuts, you know?"

"Welcome to the world of parenting a teenager," I said, laughing. "Nothing will ever be good enough from now on."

Sophia sighed and sipped her coffee. "I had really hoped for some biscuits. When that smell hit my face as I walked in, I was so happy. Your biscuits are the best."

"I'm sorry," I said. "Next time, I'll make sure to set some aside for you."

Sophia leaned back in her chair. "You said the doctor was here. Is someone sick?"

"Victor," I said, drinking my coffee. My stomach made a noise, and I realized I was already on cup number four, and it wasn't even noon yet. I had to slow down a little. My stomach couldn't deal with as much caffeine as it used to. "But it turned out to be nothing. He was cold; that's all. I think he just didn't want to go to school today. He ran away from school yesterday. I don't think he likes it there."

Sophia shivered slightly. "It is kind of cold in here."

"I know," I said and rubbed my arm. I had put on an extra sweater, but it didn't really help much. "I cranked up the radiators to their max, and it's still cold. I wonder if something is broken."

"So, what did the doctor say? Did you talk about the guy from yesterday?" Sophia asked.

I nodded. "Get this. He was frozen, completely frozen from the inside, his organs, his blood, everything. The doctor says he doesn't see how it is possible that he was still alive when he bumped into me. His temperature was zero degrees. He was frozen from the inside out."

Sophia's eyes grew wide, and she put down her cup. "What? How is that possible?"

I shrugged. "Dr. Williamsen said he didn't know. He's

gonna ask for help from Copenhagen to find out if they have an explanation."

"Wow," Sophia said pensively. "It almost sounds like black frost, but I thought that was just in plants."

"What is black frost?"

"That's what they call it when plants sort of freeze from the inside, then whither up and die. It happened to my roses last year—turned them all black. I got so mad. My mom planted those for me, and I absolutely loved them."

I swallowed my coffee and looked at Sophia pensively.

"Black frost, huh?"

"Yeah, it's not actually black, but it turns the plant black, and then it dies. Say, do you mind if I grab a blanket from the living room? I am freezing like crazy here."

"No, of course not. Grab one for me as well. It does feel like the temperature just dropped again. I don't know what's wrong."

Sophia got up from the chair and walked to the door leading to the living room. As she opened it, she stopped with a small shriek. "Oh, dear God, Victor. I didn't see you standing there. You scared me."

SEVENTEEN

Maya's shift ended at two, and she grabbed her bike that she had left leaning up against the wall behind the gas station. It had started to snow again, making it hard to bike on the sidewalk, and she had to push it instead. She was freezing and wet and so tired after having to wake up so early in the morning.

Life after high school wasn't all it was cracked up to be. It was great not to have to do a bunch of homework when she finally came home, but it was still a lot tougher than she had expected it to be. Her boss at the gas station was on her case because she wasn't working fast enough when filling the shelves in the morning, and today he had yelled at her for spilling a soda all over the floor. It was an accident, she had told him, but he didn't care.

"This is not like your home. There's no crying for momma," he had hissed at her. "Now, clean it up."

Once she finished cleaning up the spilled soda, he had been on her case the rest of the day, yelling at her for not being fast enough or for not taking care of a customer at the counter when he had just asked her to fill up the shelves with more bags of chips. There was no pleasing him, no matter how hard she tried.

And he was right. This was nothing like her home. Maya's mom would never yell at her like that.

Maya sighed and pushed the bike through a pile of snow. It was so thick it went through her trousers and soaked her. Maya shivered. She was so hungry and so tired; she just wanted to go home and lay in her bed under her covers and take a nap. Alex was going to stop by later on, he had said. She was looking forward to that. It was the highlight of her day, to be perfectly honest. Alex wasn't doing so well at home; he couldn't stand being around his dad since his mom died and his younger brother ran away, so he came to her house a lot. Maya didn't mind. It was only the hiding of Daniel that bothered her. She hated lying to Alex, and she hated the fear that came with it— the fear of losing him.

Gosh, I am so tired. I hope I won't fall asleep while he's there.

Maya exhaled, finally making it through the thick pile, and came out to an area that had been cleared of snow. Here, she could get on her bike again. Just as she sat in the saddle and put her feet on the pedals, she heard a sound that made her stop and jump off her bike again.

"Hello?"

Her voice echoed back to her. She turned her head toward a garden where she believed the sound had come from.

What was it? Someone crying? Moaning? Or could it have been just the wind?

Maya stayed still for a few seconds, listening. She didn't hear anything anymore, but something inside her told her she had to go check it out. For her own peace of mind, if nothing else.

"Hello?" she asked again, then approached an old shed on a property. She knew no one lived there, as it had been for sale for months. "Is someone here?"

The door to the shed in the front garden was left ajar, and

she walked up to it, then pulled it open. The door creaked like it was as tired as she felt.

"Hello?"

As the door opened and light spread inside the shed, she spotted the child. He was lying on his side, arms under his head like he was sleeping. Maya gasped and approached him. She put a hand on his arm but had to remove it fast. He was freezing to the touch, and it hurt her fingers.

"Are you okay, little boy?" she whispered, fear clenching her stomach. She knelt next to him when she saw the black patches, as they spread across the skin on his neck.

EIGHTEEN

I drove through the snow, while flakes the size of my hand danced in front of my windscreen. It was already turning dark. If it was the heavy snow-filled clouds lingering above the entire island or if it was already the afternoon darkness that had settled, I didn't know. I didn't care either. I was way too busy calming my daughter down on the phone while driving to her.

She had called while I was in the living room, starting the fireplace, trying desperately to heat the house. Victor was freezing, and Sophia had ended up leaving because she thought it was too cold in my house. Daniel had been chattering his teeth as well when he came down for a snack, and I gave him one of Victor's old sweaters that he never wore. I told Daniel to sit by the fireplace while I started the fire.

That's when my phone had rung. It was Maya, screaming in desperation. I told her to call Morten and then call me back. Now, she was guiding me toward the house, and I parked outside of the beech hedge surrounding the property. It was the most common sort of hedge around here. It was pretty in the spring and the summer, but not so much during the wintertime. The leaves had fallen off, and its bare branches were bent with the weight of the snow. In the front garden, I could only see half of the for sale sign as it poked out of a pile of snow.

"Maya?" I called and walked across the driveway to the shed in the front garden that the former owners had probably used for parking their bikes and putting away garden tools.

"In here, Mom. In here!"

I walked inside and found her next to a young boy, who lay lifeless on some old tarp that the previous owners had left in there.

"What happened?"

"I... I don't know. I was passing by on my bike, on my way home, when I heard something. It sounded like a child crying. I stopped to see what it was and found him. He's freezing cold. I tried to touch him to feel for a pulse, but it hurt my fingers. What's wrong with him, Mom? His skin seems to be turning black."

My heart hammering in my throat, I reached over and touched him to turn him around. Immediately, I had to recoil because it sent a shock of pain through my fingers the second my skin touched his. That's how cold he was.

"Is he... is he...?" Maya asked, half crying behind me.

The boy moved, and I shook my head. "He's still alive."

In the distance, I could hear sirens, and I rushed out just as Morten and the ambulance driven by Mrs. Williamsen pulled up. She opened the back, and the doctor jumped out.

"Hurry, he's still alive," I said. "But barely."

As the doctor passed me, I grabbed his arm gently. Our eyes locked for a brief second. "He's freezing cold, and his skin is turning black."

The doctor gave me a nod that told me he understood. He was wearing thick gloves like he already knew.

"We've got him from here."

Morten gave me a quick glare, then a nervous smile, before he rushed in with them. Seconds later, they rolled the boy out on a stretcher. Morten came up behind me and placed a hand on my shoulder. I turned to face him, and the hand soon became awkward, so he removed it.

"Still can't seem to stay out of trouble, huh?"

I shook my head and moved away, so we didn't stand so close.

Being near him reminded me of how broken my heart was over our breakup. I was trying so hard to forget him, but every time I saw him, it all came back.

"It's not exactly the time for jokes, Morten. Not when we just sent off a young boy fighting for his life. I can't deal with that right now. It's inappropriate."

He lowered his eyes. "You're right. I am sorry."

"His name is Jannik," I said with a sniffle, breaking the silence between us. "The boy's name is. Just thought I'd save you some time figuring out who he was."

"You know him?" he asked and pulled out a notepad, then scribbled down the name in that unreadable handwriting of his. I often wondered how on earth he could read it himself when the day was over. "Do you have a last name?"

I shook my head and avoided looking directly at him. I was scared he'd see how much I missed him. I didn't want him to know.

"Nope. But he's full-time at Fishy Pines. He's in Victor's class—you'll probably find he ran away from there if you call and check. Thinking of how frozen this boy was, he might have been staying in the shed for some time, just thought you should know. See you around."

I grabbed Maya by the hand, and we walked to the car together. I strapped her bike to the back, and we both got in. I slammed the door shut, then sat for a few seconds, gathering myself before I was ready to leave. I focused on breathing properly to calm myself.

Maya placed a hand on my arm. "Mom? Are you all right? You look kind of pale."

I looked out the windscreen and caught a glimpse of Morten as he got back into his patrol car and started the engine. I sniffled and nodded, forcing myself to smile, even though I most of all wanted to cry. Or scream. Maybe both. I hated seeing him when I missed him so terribly. He looked like he was doing a little too well without me, and it saddened me.

How was he coping so well with this breakup when I was left so devastated? Why wasn't he awake at night crying? Why didn't he pick up his phone six times a day, wanting to text me, as I did for him? Was I that easy to forget? Was it really that effortless to move on after me? The thoughts were crushing.

"I will be," I said with a deep exhale, watching him take off and disappear down the road. "Once we get home and get warmed up. Maybe get some hot chocolate, how about that?"

"Sounds good," Maya said, her voice breaking slightly. She thought I didn't notice and cleared her throat. I turned the heat up inside the car, and a breeze of warm air hit our frozen bodies. I welcomed it greatly as I had felt like an icicle all day.

Maya didn't speak until we drove up into our own street, and we could see our house towering at the end of it.

"Do you think the boy will make it?" she asked.

I stopped the car in our driveway and got out, avoiding having to answer her question at all costs. Because, if I was honest, no. I didn't think he would make it.

And it broke my heart in more ways than I thought possible.

NINETEEN

The next morning, it turned into a regular fight between Victor and me. He told me he didn't want to go to the school again, ever, and that's when I realized I had gotten myself a teenager on my hands. He dismissed any argument I brought forth and refused even to listen to a word I said.

He went to his room, then slammed the door shut, and I stood back, not knowing what to do. I watched the school bus from Fishy Pines come and go, then sat down in the kitchen, preparing myself for the phone call I was about to receive from HP. It didn't come.

I drank coffee and decided to wait a little longer while going over the speech in my mind that I wanted to give him to defend myself. As the call still didn't come, I read the article in the local paper about Jannik, the boy who had been found in a shed. It was just a small note, as there were other things going on here on the island that were more important.

Our dear mayor, Lisa Rasmussen, had held a press conference the day before, and that filled the rest of the paper. Apparently, she was expecting delegations from China, Russia, and North Korea to arrive in a few days, and she had some big surprise for us islanders that would blow our minds. Those were her words in the paper, "blow our minds."

It made me very concerned. I knew she was up for reelection, and, of course, she wanted to make her mark, and hopefully be remembered for something big, but this worried me more than I'd expected. Mostly because I knew Lisa very well and knew she was capable of many things. She would go to great lengths to get reelected, and that wasn't a good thing in my book.

"What are you up to now, Lisa?" I mumbled while reading the rest of the article, where the mayor talked about this big new thing that she was working on and had been for years, and now it would finally pay off, but it was too early for her to reveal the details.

I couldn't help wondering why it was those countries that were sending delegations. Why weren't any European countries invited? It wasn't usually those countries that we as a nation would do business with. Something smelled fishy about this.

I sighed and put the paper down, then finished my coffee and looked at the clock. It was almost noon, and HP hadn't called yet, which made me think that maybe he just believed that Victor was still sick. I had the doctor's note from the day before to prove it, so I guess I was okay. The note said he should stay at home the day before, not today, but maybe I could argue that he had gotten worse overnight. Yes, that would be my argument for at least a couple of days.

Victor took a turn for the worse.

Satisfied at this, I rose to my feet and cleaned my cup, then stared at my phone. I knew I shouldn't, but I couldn't help myself. I called Dr. Williamsen's number.

"Emma?" he said, sounding surprised. "What can I do for you? Is Victor okay?"

"He's good; I mean, he stayed at home today as well, but..."

"Emma, he needs to go to school. If he doesn't have a fever, he really should go."

That made me feel bad. Like I had done something wrong. I had hoped the doctor would have my back on this.

"He will eventually. But that's not why I called. How's the boy?" I asked. "I can't stop thinking about him. Is he going to make it?"

A deep sigh followed. It wasn't a pleasant one. It had the heaviness of a deeply worried man in it.

"To be honest, I don't know. He isn't conscious. But at least he's still breathing."

"That's good to hear. How's his condition?" I asked.

"Well, to tell you the truth, this is a first for me. His body temperature is very low, dangerously low, ranging in the teens, and I don't understand how he is not dead yet. He is barely hanging on. We're trying to warm him up here at the clinic, but with no luck so far. I wanted to take him to the hospital on the mainland, but the ocean froze over during the night, so they can't come here to pick him up. I don't know what is getting to this place these days. It's getting colder around here. We don't usually see these freezing temperatures already in November."

"How long had he been in that shed, do you think?" I asked, concerned, thinking that maybe that was why I was constantly so cold inside my house as well. Perhaps it was just getting colder all over the place.

"That's the odd part. Fishy Pines said he ran away yesterday. They had people looking for him. Now, they want him back, saying they have their own doctors on hand, but I am not letting him go anywhere until his body temperature is up to normal. In the end, it's the parents' decision. So far, they haven't decided on where they want the boy treated, so I won't budge until they say the word."

"Good for you," I said. "You shouldn't."

I hung up with the doctor, then felt myself shiver with cold, just as Victor entered the kitchen. As he brushed past me to grab a soda from the cabinet, I felt a wave of freezing cold hit me.

"Victor, are you all right?" I asked and rubbed my arms to get warmth in them.

He didn't answer, just grabbed the soda and walked past me. As he did, I noticed the soda in his hand was cracking.

"Give me that," I said to my son, then pulled it out from between his fingers. The bottle was completely frozen, and the contents inside were solid. I stared at my son in front of me, then grabbed his hands in mine. Just standing close to him made me tremble with cold.

"Victor, what's going on? You're freezing."

"I told you I was cold," he said, his purple lips vibrating.

"Oh, dear God," I said and grabbed a blanket from a chair, then wrapped him in it.

"We need you warmed up, pronto."

TWENTY

"Hello there. You're new. I'm Thomas."

A pale man with ruby red lips smiled at Ingrid. She glanced around her and looked at the people who were standing in the living room, chatting, with cups of coffee or tea in their hands. They didn't look as crazy as Ingrid had expected them to be. There were a couple of teenagers there too, a little older than her, but not by much. She smiled awkwardly at one of them, and he smiled back, then looked at his feet.

"I'm... Ingrid," she said, feeling silly.

What am I doing here?

She glanced up at the banner on the wall reading FANOE ISLAND UFO RESEARCH AND EXPERIENCES GROUP.

"Welcome, Ingrid. How did you hear about us?" Thomas asked.

"Umm, Facebook. I found your group and read the stories there."

She felt her heart beat faster as a guy standing next to her rubbed his hair excessively, almost manically, then jerked his head sideways while making a loud whistling noise with his mouth.

Thomas saw her staring.

"That's John. Don't worry about the head jerking. He's got Tourette's. It has nothing to do with why he is here. He can't control it. His story is interesting, though. But I bet yours is too, am I right?" He tilted his head. She hated the way he looked at her like he knew her secret or something. She felt like leaving. These people were just as weird as she had feared they would be.

"Coffee?" Thomas asked.

She smiled while glaring toward the door.

"Maybe I should..."

He placed a hand on her shoulder. She turned to look at him, then at his hand. He removed it, then rubbed his hands together and blew on them, like he was suddenly cold. His smile was warm as he looked at her.

"We all had trouble with this the first time. Sharing these types of stories with others can be a daunting experience. But it can also help to talk about it with like-minded people who have experienced something similar."

"But that's the thing," Ingrid said. "I don't know whether that's what happened to me or not. Everyone thinks I'm crazy."

He laughed. "They usually do. Say, are you cold? You're shivering."

She nodded. "I am freezing."

"It is cold out today, and in here too now that I think about it. Maybe someone left the front door open; I'll have to check on that. I'll get you a blanket to warm you up." He rubbed his hands together and shuddered lightly, then pointed toward the circle of chairs. "Come, let's sit down, and then you can decide if our little group is for you or not. If not, then no harm done, okay?"

Ingrid stared at the twenty chairs shaping a circle in the middle of the living room. From the outside, the place had looked like any house on Fanoe island. She had passed it many times on her bike and never known what went on inside. She didn't know what she had expected, maybe a cabin in the woods, or some small, strange house hidden by thorn bushes.

You're nuts. Of course, it's just a normal house with normal people—people who've had abnormal experiences just like you.

Would she have to tell them her story? Would she dare to?

"Here's your coffee," Thomas said and handed her a cup. "You can sit next to Tony over there. He'll take good care of you."

Ingrid grabbed the cup, then went to sit down, glancing cautiously at the man Thomas had placed her next to. She smiled nervously. Tony leaned forward, and she sipped her coffee, hoping it would warm her up slightly. Still, it felt like the more she drank, the colder she felt inside, and soon everyone in the room was rubbing their arms and legs and complaining to Thomas that it was freezing in here.

"I don't know what to do," Thomas said, reaching out his hands. "I have turned the radiators up to full strength, and all the windows and doors are closed. I don't understand why it's still so cold in here."

He hugged himself and rubbed his shoulders when Ingrid stood to her feet. All eyes were on her as she opened her mouth and said, "I think I might be to blame for that."

TWENTY-ONE

Maya called in sick the next day. She couldn't face the world, or her annoying boss, after what had happened. She barely slept all night and kept seeing the boy lying there on the tarp in the shed, crying for help. She couldn't shake the freezing sensation she had when coming near him or how it stung her fingers when she tried to touch him. She had never felt anything like it—this extreme cold.

YOU OK?

It was from Christina, her best friend. She had texted her a thousand times the night before, and now she was at it again. It wasn't that Maya didn't want to answer her; it was just that she didn't know what to tell her.

The same went for Alex. He had been texting and calling her ever since she sent him a text canceling their plans the night before. She hadn't given him any explanation. How could she? He would start to ask questions, and she had no answers. Once she told him everything, she'd have to really tell him everything.

Including how Asgar died and Samuel, and the others, and that they had Daniel at their house.

She couldn't tell him just a little bit of the story. Daniel was a big part of what had been happening the past year or so. The mysterious creatures, Daniel's ability to turn to water, his mother roaming the sewers, her brother's strange mind powers. And now a potential virus that caused people to freeze to death.

Maya and her mom had talked about it the night before when they sat in the kitchen together. Maya's mom had told her that she had spoken to Dr. Williamsen about the guy who died in her arms and how his organs and blood froze from the inside. Her mom was convinced it was some sort of unknown virus that was killing them, causing their body temperatures to drop like that.

Either that or she was losing her mind. It was one or the other, her mother had said.

Maya texted Christina back and told her she was fine but had the flu, then did the same to Alex, buying herself some time, avoiding having to explain herself to either of them.

She then walked down the stairs and shuddered in her sweater. She crossed her arms in front of her chest as she walked into the living room, where she found her mother and Victor in front of the fireplace. Victor was wearing a thick blanket and several sweaters underneath; still, he was shivering, and his lips had turned purple.

"What's going in here?" Maya asked, her pulse quickening. She walked closer but felt colder as she did, and soon her teeth were chattering.

"It's Victor," her mom said, sounding terrified. "We can't seem to get him warmed up. He's shaking, and no matter what I do, it doesn't help him. I don't know what to do."

"How about a warm bath?" Maya asked.

"That was the first thing we did," her mother said. Maya

could hear the deep concern in the tone of her voice. Her lips quivered as she spoke. "It helped for a few minutes. But now he's colder than ever. I'm at my wit's end. What are we going to do?"

PART II

TWENTY-TWO

Tony reached into his pockets, searching for his pack of cigarettes. He pulled one out and put it between his lips, then lit it. Shaking heavily, he smoked and looked nervously around him.

Tony didn't used to be this way, this constant anxiousness and paranoia. He didn't used to smoke either. But since that day, since he was... taken... he had been so scared, especially when he—like now—walked his dog at the park at night.

Buddy, the bulldog, lifted a leg and peed on a streetlamp while Tony smoked his cigarette, constantly throwing glances around to make sure he was alone, that they didn't sneak up on him again.

It was right here in this exact spot that he had been taken the first time—while walking through the park at night with his dog. There had been a bright light, blinding him, and then he had disappeared. Buddy had run home, and, luckily for Tony, the dog was sitting by the front door when he finally made it back. But where Tony had been in between, he had no recollection. He just knew he had been gone all night and woken up naked on the beach.

As he took a shower, he saw the red swollen bumps on his shoulders. He was certain they looked like injection marks, and that's when he knew in his heart that he had been taken and experimented on. Aliens were the only sensible explanation, and after going back and forth on it for a few days, he had contacted the UFO group and attended his first meeting. Hearing the others' stories had helped immensely, but it hadn't taken away the fear of it happening again.

A few weeks later, his fear came true, and he was taken again. This time while he was driving his car on the south side of the island. A bright light had enveloped him, and he had stopped because he couldn't see. That was the last thing he could remember. Once he woke up again, he was sitting in his car with his head slumped over the steering wheel, parked on the side of the road. Now, most people would just believe they had been tired, then parked the car to sleep and dreamt the rest. But Tony knew better than that. Two marks on his other shoulder told him he had been taken once again. And it also told him the aliens weren't done with him yet.

As it turned out, he was right about that. Three weeks later, he was sitting in his garden, smoking a cigarette, when the light appeared again. It blinded him like the two times before, and after that, he didn't remember anything. He woke up in the park, sleeping on the side of the road. The police were standing by him, trying to wake him up, and he was taken to the station to sleep it off. He tried to explain what had happened, but they laughed and told him they believed he had to be wasted to tell a story like that.

The only ones who had ever believed him were the people in his UFO group. All of them had similar experiences, and at the last meeting, the new girl had told a story so close to his, even that it happened at the same park, that it had made him both angry and relieved at the same time. Relieved because he wasn't alone, yet angry because this was still going on, and there was nothing they could do to stop it. There were no laws to protect them and no one to believe their stories. How many more needed to be abducted before they would be taken seriously?

UFOs were real, and aliens experimented on people from this island. How were people so narrow-minded that they didn't believe it? With so many people telling the same story? Tony finished his cigarette and crushed it on the asphalt when he heard a rustle in the bushes behind him and felt a shiver go through his body. He was reminded of the story that the new girl had told—that she was constantly freezing after her abduction and how she had frozen things that she touched. She had also claimed that it was her fault that the house had turned freezing after she entered. It was truly fascinating to Tony. He had never heard of this phenomenon before, but, of course, the aliens could do that too.

They were capable of everything and would stop at nothing.

Tony sighed, then looked down at Buddy.

"Come on, it's getting late," he said to the white bulldog. "You know I don't like to be in the park this late. Let's go home."

Tony turned around to start walking back when a bright light encompassed him and blinded him completely. Tony screamed and sank to his knees, letting go of the leash and the dog. Buddy took off, running down the trail, the leash dangling on the asphalt behind it.

Scared, Tony folded his hands in prayer and yelled at the top of his lungs, "PLEASE! NOT AGAIN! PLEASE! NOT AGAIN!"

TWENTY-THREE

Dinner at the Finnerup house was quite different from what Maya was used to at her house. Where her family was rowdy and someone always talking, often several at the same time, sometimes arguing, other times just laughing, Alex's house was quiet, and his dad barely uttered a word during the entire dinner.

They ate in the big dining room at their house, sitting underneath the chandelier, his dad at the end of the big mahogany table, sipping his wine, a sound that normally wouldn't be heard if there had been other noises in the room, but there weren't.

Maya cleared her throat and chewed a piece of the lamb. Alex's dad, Christopher Finnerup, looked at her, and she wondered if she had made too much noise. Was she chewing too loudly? Or was she sitting in a wrong way? Was she not dressed nicely enough for his house?

He sipped his wine from the crystal glass that the armoire behind him was filled to the brim with. He splashed it around inside his mouth a few times before he finally swallowed it, then looked at her again.

Then he spoke. His voice echoed against the walls behind them.

"Say... Maya... you've been hanging out here a lot lately. You and Alex have. Are things okay at home?"

Maya stopped chewing. She stared at the man. His stern look made her feel like she was lying to him, even though she hadn't said a word.

"It's just that," Alex said, "her house is really cold these days. So, we've been hanging out here the past few days instead."

"Cold? How so? Doesn't your heat work?" Dr. Finnerup asked.

Maya shook her head and swallowed the bite she had in her mouth. She held a hand up in front of her mouth to make sure he couldn't see food inside of it when she spoke.

"No, it actually works really well. It's just, well, my brother is freezing cold, and somehow he seems to make the entire house cold."

Dr. Finnerup stared at her, food still in his mouth. He had stopped chewing while his eyes lingered on her.

"It's hard to explain," she said, feeling like she had told him too much. She was just so sick of lying to this family who had been nothing but nice to her. She had told Alex about Victor, also about the kid she had found in the shed. She hadn't told him he was frozen, just that he was almost dead, and she had found him, and that was why she had been feeling sick.

She had told him this after dodging his calls for a day or so and then decided this wasn't getting her anywhere good. This would end up destroying her relationship with Alex if she didn't at least tell him some of what was going on. She'd just have to leave out the part about Daniel being in her house. She also hated not telling Dr. Finnerup. She knew Daniel wasn't his biological son. But still. He had raised him, hadn't he?

Yet she had made a promise to her mother, and she was honoring it for as long as possible.

"We think it might be a virus or something. Something new that the doctors haven't figured out what it is yet. Hopefully, he'll beat it soon, and we can go back to normal."

"So, you're saying he's freezing, huh?" Dr. Finnerup asked. "And because of it, the entire house is cold too. So much so that you can't stand being there and come here instead."

Maya nodded but didn't feel good. Had she said too much? Her heart sank when realizing she probably had. She didn't care for the look in Dr. Finnerup's eyes as he pointed at her with his fork.

"Very interesting, Miss Frost. Very interesting indeed."

TWENTY-FOUR

In the following couple of days, Victor didn't improve much, but he didn't get worse either. Dr. Williamsen stopped by every morning to check his temperature, and it was lingering about twenty-seven degrees, which was low and alarming. Yet Dr. Williamsen noted that Victor seemed fine otherwise. He was freezing, yes, and complaining about it, but he was responsive, and actually didn't seem sick at all. He would spend the day by the fireplace, drawing, reading comics, or playing video games, Daniel and Brutus by his side. He was the same old Victor. Nothing indicated that he was in any way sick.

Meanwhile, I didn't seem to be able to warm up the house anymore, and I walked around in several sweaters, carrying blankets with me everywhere I went, shivering beneath them, teeth chattering. I hadn't written anything on my latest book because every time I sat down to my computer, my hands were so cold, I couldn't stand touching the keyboard. I still had the radiators on max heat, and when I put my hand on one of them, it was burning hot, so it wasn't that they didn't work. It was just like they weren't enough somehow.

It was like the cold emerging from Victor was overpowering it.

I shook my head while thinking this, then placed my behind on one of the radiators and let it heat me up. I closed my eyes as I felt the burning heat and enjoyed a few seconds of warmth. The nighttime was the worst, and last night I had barely slept because I was freezing so terribly.

I had been wondering what to do about Victor, and how to make him better, how to stop this. Dr. Williamsen had no idea how to deal with it, and he had called and asked his colleagues in Copenhagen, but even the experts had never heard of a disease that caused people to freeze like this. He had Jannik at his clinic and still had no luck healing him either. He was alive, but only barely hanging on. At the same time, the frost seemed to have gotten a firm grip on our island as the ocean around us was frozen so solidly that we had been cut off from the world. At least until the icebreakers got here, but that could take days.

"Do you want to play cards?" Daniel asked Victor.

My behind was beginning to burn, so I removed myself from the radiator and wrapped myself tightly with the blanket, then walked back into the kitchen where I had the cooker on with bread inside of it. The smell pleased my nostrils. I loved baking, and since our house had been like a frozen tundra, I had been running the cooker constantly in the hope that it might help heat the house a little bit. But the only heat I felt was when I stood right next to it, or when I opened the door and checked on my bread.

It was no secret that I was getting pretty tired of this freezing cold, and as Sophia came over and Kenneth barked at her, then bit into her shoe with her foot still in it, I hugged her, just to feel the warmth she brought with her.

"Warm me, please," I said, teeth chattering again.

Sophia laughed and rubbed my back. She felt so nice and warm that I wanted to stay in her embrace forever.

"Smells good in here," she said and let go of me. I shuddered again while she added, "But it always does."

"I think the bread is done. Let's get some coffee. Warm, burning hot coffee."

I reached down and got ahold of Kenneth, who refused to let go of her shoe until I pulled at his collar. Alma staggered into the living room, where she found the boys and Brutus. I heard them sigh, annoyed at the sight of the little girl who would most definitely ruin everything.

"I take it Victor isn't getting any better," Sophia said. She was about to take off her winter coat, then decided against it when she felt the coldness of my house. I wondered how long we could keep meeting at my house, or if she'd stop coming because of it. Sophia didn't have much room at her place, and, with six kids, she wasn't fond of having people over.

"It's odd, though," I said pensively. "He seems fine otherwise. He's being himself completely, even with all his oddness. It's just that he's so incredibly cold all the time. And sometimes when he touches things, they turn to ice. I have him wear gloves so he can play Xbox without destroying the thing."

"What does the school say?" Sophia asked, lifting her eyebrows. "Are they okay with him not going? I know they were on your case about his absence just a few weeks ago."

I shrugged and served her a cup of hot coffee. She grabbed it, and I cut the warm steaming bread, then buttered a piece. I poured some coffee in my cup too and held it between my hands to warm them. Between the newly baked bread and the steaming coffee, I felt almost normal. Well, almost.

"I don't know actually, and I'm not sure I care. I haven't heard from them since I called in and said he was sick. I guess they must have given up. I think I am doing the right thing by keeping him at home. I mean, Dr. Williamsen says he believes Victor can go to school just fine, but I really don't think they'll want him there. Everywhere he goes, everything becomes freezing cold. And he might be contagious. I'm not sending him there until we know what is wrong with him. He might even have gotten it at the school in the first place."

"Because of that other kid?"

I nodded and swallowed my coffee. It burned my tongue, but I didn't mind. It felt good as it warmed me on the way down.

"Jannik," I said. "But that is exactly what I'm afraid of. What if it is some disease, some strange new virus that we haven't heard of or seen before, then I am pretty sure this dude gave it to Victor. We don't know if Victor might give it to someone else if he goes back there. No, I think it's best to keep him here for now. It's safer for everyone. I think they'll understand that. They'll have to."

Sophia sipped her coffee. She seemed to think about it for a few seconds, then smiled.

"You're probably right. Plus, if they're not bothering you about it, then I'm sure it's fine. You'll be just fine. I wouldn't worry. I mean, what can they possibly do to you?"

TWENTY-FIVE

Ingrid whistled happily as she rode her bike down the street. Today was a good day. School had been awful, but it was Thursday, and that was when the UFO group met at Thomas's house. She was looking forward to seeing her friends again—the only people who knew what she was going through.

Ever since her first meeting with them, she had been so relieved. It was like she was carrying this tremendous secret, and she knew no one would believe her. But once she met these people for the first time, everything changed. Their stories were so similar to hers, and they understood the confusion that followed.

Now, it was time for her parents to know.

Ingrid had discussed it with her group at their last meeting and told them she wanted to tell her parents what she believed really happened to her. The group had encouraged her to go ahead and told her it was the best thing to do, instead of keeping it a secret. But they had also said that she had to prepare herself for them not to believe her.

"They might even laugh," Thomas had warned. "That's what happened to many of us here."

The group had nodded, and Ingrid knew they were right. Yet she still wanted to break it to her parents. She was tired of lying to them, of hiding this big part of herself and her life from them.

"Mom, Dad?" she asked as she rushed in through the front door. Her mother was sitting in the kitchen, looking at her phone, finger scrolling. She looked up, and her eyes met Ingrid's. She smiled.

"Oh, hi, sweetie. How was your day?"

Ingrid didn't want to answer that. School had been awful lately, and she had a hard time sitting still in class because she was freezing so terribly. She also hated going because her friends had all turned their backs on her, and she felt so lonely all the time. She could hear them as they whispered behind her back when passing them in the hallway. But she didn't want her mother to know all this. She had enough worries as it was. So, she didn't answer. She looked around her.

"Where's Dad?"

"In the office."

Ingrid knew her parents both worked from home on Thursdays; that was why she had chosen today to tell them. That and because she had a meeting tonight and she wanted to tell the group how she finally managed to tell her parents. They were going to be so proud of her.

Ingrid knocked on the door to the office.

"Yes?"

She opened the door and peeked inside. "Dad? You busy?"

He sighed and looked at the pile of papers towering next to him. "Kind of. What's up?"

"I want to talk to you and Mom. Can you come to the living room, please? It's important."

Ingrid's dad exhaled deeply and rubbed his receding hairline. "Can't it wait? I'm pretty swamped here."

"It's important, Dad. Please?"

He pushed his office chair back. "All right. I guess work can wait. Nothing's more important than my girl."

Ingrid smiled. "Thanks, Dad. It means the world to me."

TWENTY-SIX

The car drove up in my driveway late in the afternoon. It was dark out already, and I was preparing chicken for dinner when I spotted it. Morten's patrol car drove up right behind it. Seeing him as he got out made my heart drop.

What's he doing here? What's he doing with these men?

A group of men wearing long black coats and big boots got out of the back of the black SUV. The front door opened, and someone else got out as well, and that's when I became more puzzled than ever.

HP?

"You're kidding me," I mumbled, then got extremely nervous. I heard the doorbell ring, then hurried to open the door.

"Morten? What are you doing here?" I asked, heart already pounding in my chest. HP and the men in black coats kept in the background. HP didn't even look at me.

"HP?" I said, lips quivering. "What's going on?"

Morten gave me a look, and I knew this was serious. "I'm sorry, Emma. I don't have a choice."

I stared at him, the man I loved so dearly. Right now, I wanted to punch him in the face.

"You don't have a choice? What's that supposed to mean?"

He swallowed. This was unpleasant for him. "These men are here to pick up Victor."

"Victor? What do you mean? I don't understand, Morten; what's going on here? Last time I checked, Victor was my son."

"They have a court order, Emma," he said. "My hands are tied. I have to help them. Social services is involved."

"Excuse me? Involved in what?"

He closed his eyes briefly, then looked at me again. "They're taking Victor. They're admitting him full-time to Fishy Pines."

I shook my head. "No, they're not. He's my son, and he's not going anywhere. Least of all to that awful place."

"You're not listening, Emma. They have a court order. They're allowed to take him. It's for his own good."

"For his own good? What's that supposed to mean?"

"He needs treatment, Emma, and you know it very well. We have been extremely patient with you, but that is over now," HP said and took over, stepping forward. "You've been holding him back, keeping him at home. You're obstructing his treatment and his schooling. He hasn't been to school this entire week, and even before that, he was hardly ever there, Emma. He needs to go to school; it's the law. And a boy with his... condition needs treatment. And you can't provide what he needs. That's why he'll be admitted full-time, so we can observe him."

I glared at HP, then at Morten, who looked like he wanted to hide in a hole somewhere.

"Morten, you can't let them do this. You know how Victor needs to be with me. Besides, he's been sick. That's why he hasn't been to school. You can ask Dr. Williamsen."

"They did, Emma. He said the boy is capable of going to school."

"But he's not... I know my son... something's wrong with him. You can't take a sick child."

"I am a doctor," HP said. "If anything is wrong with Victor, he'll receive the treatment he needs. Now, please bring us the boy."

I stared at him, nostrils flaring, then at Morten.

"I don't..."

"Have a choice," I said. "I get it."

"You should just be happy that they're not taking him away from you completely," he said. "Social services was talking about it, but I talked them out of it. I said you'd be cooperative, and you only wanted what was best for Victor. At least now, he'll still come back to you once his treatment ends, Emma."

Morten grabbed my arm while saying the last part. I felt so betrayed by him that I wanted to scream. Instead, I stared into his eyes, mine filling with tears.

"But... I can't live without him."

"You don't have to," Morten said. "You can see him during visiting hours, and he'll come home... at some point later on. This is your only option. If you don't hand him over to these men, they'll take him away from you completely. So, don't try anything stupid, Emma."

"I can't believe you'd do this to me," I hissed at Morten as I pulled my arm away and slammed the door shut in his face. I wasn't going to let these men take my son. There was no way. I'd hide him in the basement, then take him to the mainland at nighttime as soon as it was possible to sail across the water, once the icebreakers had made their way through. Heck, I'd walk on the ice if I had to. There was no way I was losing my son to these people. No way.

I turned around on my heel when someone opened the door

behind me. I turned with a gasp. It was one of the men in black coats.

"Ma'am. We need the boy. Now."

Behind him, three more of them came up and pushed me aside, while I yelled at Victor:

"Victor, get out of here. Now!"

There was turmoil, and I was being held back by a big goon, while I could hear my son screaming from the living room. The sound made me panic. The guy's big arm was holding me back, so I sank my teeth into his wrist and bit with all I had.

He roared and pulled away his arm, making room for me to be able to run through the hallway.

"Victor!"

I pulled the door open to the living room just as two men came toward me, carrying a screaming Victor. He was kicking and squirming in their arms but unable to get loose. For once, I wanted him to use his powers, the same powers he used to blow up the gates of the school, but he didn't. He had told me a long time ago that he was afraid to hurt someone, so that's why he never did when there were people close to him. He was scared of his own strength.

"Victor!" I yelled as they came toward me. One of them reached out his hand and pushed me to the side as I tried to grab for my son.

"MOM!" he yelled, reaching out his hands toward me, but I couldn't help him. It was devastating because I felt so helpless.

"Victor!" I yelled back as they opened the front door and walked out with him. Victor grabbed the door but could only hold on for a few seconds.

Screaming and kicking, they carried him to the car and put him in. Seconds later, they took off, leaving me standing on the doorstep, screaming my son's name.

Crying, I placed my forehead on the door, then looked at

where Victor had held on to it and realized it was covered in white frost. It had left a perfect print of Victor's hand on the wood.

TWENTY-SEVEN

"Okay. Here's the deal."

Ingrid and her parents had sat down in the living room on the old leather couches they'd had since they were just married. Her mother had asked if she wanted some tea or a biscuit or anything, but Ingrid had said no. She needed to do it now, and she needed to do it fast before she chickened out.

I can do it. Just say it.

Her parents' eyes were on her, and it made her even more nervous. She rubbed her hands together to make them stop shaking. She was so cold, but she couldn't think about that now.

"I... have been abducted by aliens."

Ingrid said the words, much to her own surprise. She heard them leave her lips, then felt her tongue turn into a knot. She paused and waited to see if there would be a reaction, then continued as she had planned. "Now, before you say that you don't believe me, let me just tell you that I am not the only one. Several people on the island have experienced it. Now, I don't know many details, but I do know that I disappeared, and I was taken somewhere, and I'm pretty sure I was experimented on.

Again, others have experienced the same thing. I am not the only one."

A long pause followed. Ingrid felt her beating heart pound while wondering if she should say something else. When neither of her parents uttered a single word, she continued.

"Okay... think about this. Have you noticed that the house is freezing cold lately? And that I am always cold? Well, it's because of me. The aliens did something to me, put something inside of me that makes me freeze constantly. I think they injected something into me, but I don't know what or why. I do know that it has changed my blood, so it has a different color; it's more yellow, almost green."

Still crickets.

No one made a noise. Her mom was about to, but then stopped herself. Ingrid went into the kitchen, grabbed a knife, and came back. "Here, I can show you."

She placed the knife on the skin of her arm to cut it open like they had all done at the group meeting, realizing that they all had changed blood. Some had green; others more yellow like hers. It was when seeing this that Ingrid had finally realized she was like them—that they weren't crazy. That whatever happened to them had happened to her too.

Finally, her mom reacted when seeing the knife on her skin. She rose to her feet and reached out her hand. "No!"

Ingrid looked up. Her mother smiled. It seemed forced. Her shoulders came down a little.

"It's okay. We believe you; don't we, Jacob?"

Her dad looked at Ingrid. He too had risen to his feet and had a terrified look on his face.

"Just hand the knife to your mother, will you? Nice and quiet. There's no need to do anything rash here. Just give her the knife, and we'll talk, okay?"

Ingrid stared at her parents. They seemed terrified.

"Okay," she said and placed the knife on the coffee table.

Her mother rushed to it, grabbed it, then ran to the kitchen with the knife in her hand, holding it like she feared it might explode. She scrambled with something... it sounded almost like she was taking all the knives and placing them in a drawer. Then, she returned.

"Okay. That's done."

Ingrid wrinkled her forehead. "I see. But can I tell you more about my experience now and the group I have been going to? Because I really want you to be a part of it."

Her mother nodded nervously, then smiled. "Of course, sweetie. Of course. Come, let's sit on the couch again, and we'll talk. I want to hear everything about it."

Ingrid felt puzzled. Was her mom actually trying here? It seemed like it. This was a great surprise to her, as she had expected them to get mad or tell her she was crazy. But neither of them seemed like they believed she was. They seemed genuinely interested.

Ingrid sat down with a relieved sigh. Silly her for judging her parents like that. She looked from one to the other. Her mom took her hands in hers, then shivered from the cold wave that went through her.

"Does this mean... that you actually believe me?" Ingrid said.

Her parents looked at each other, then nodded simultaneously. "Of course, we believe you, sweetie. Of course, we do."

Her dad threw out his arms with a laugh. "Why wouldn't we? It's not that hard to believe that our daughter was abducted by aliens, is it?"

TWENTY-EIGHT

"And they just took him?"

Sophia looked up at me from above her wineglass. I had called her right after they left with Victor, and we had opened a bottle of wine. I was trying desperately to drown out the screaming voices inside my head, telling me I had messed everything up—that I was a failure and unable to be a decent mother to my own child.

I let it go too far. It could have been avoided.

I nodded. "How did I let it go this far? Why didn't I listen when they threatened to admit him? Now, he has to be there full-time, and he hates that place."

"I can't believe they can do this. They can't just take a child from its mother. What has it come to?"

I exhaled, trying to suppress the panic erupting inside me when thinking about my son and realizing I had no idea when I'd see him again. How was I supposed to go on without him? How would I survive this?

"I had a friend who had her daughter taken by social services," Sophia said and poured us both some more red wine in our glasses. My head was spinning out of control, and it didn't feel like the wine was helping anything. On the contrary, I felt more confused now than ever. "She didn't see her child for three years before they finally figured out that it was a mistake. It was all based on what some teacher had said to them, and the teacher had a grudge against my friend because she didn't want to sleep with him. It was an ugly deal, but eventually, she got her daughter back."

"After three years?" I said, almost spitting out the words. "I can't wait that long. Heaven knows what they'll do to him during that time."

"No, of course not. My friend's daughter had lived three years with a foster family and came back a completely different child. She had been abused by the dad it turned out."

I put my glass down and sent Sophia a look. She wrinkled her nose.

"I'm not helping, am I? Sorry. I'll keep my mouth shut."

I exhaled and shook my head slowly. "No, you're just trying to help. I'm just... well, a little sensitive right now. There's a reason Victor doesn't want to go to that place. There's a reason he keeps running away. And now he is doomed to stay there full-time. I can't believe it."

Sophia put her hand in mine. "We'll get him out of there. Somehow. What about that lawyer of yours? The one who helped you with trying to get Skye out of Omicon? Michael something?"

I sighed. "He's not my lawyer anymore."

"Maybe he'll take this case. I'm sure it's not as complicated as looking for a child no one thinks even exists."

I nodded and looked into my glass of wine. "True. I just... I'll try him. I'll do anything to get my boy back."

I sipped my wine again when my phone vibrated. I looked at the display with a sniffle while thinking about my poor son in that awful place. Was he crying? Was he calling my name?

"It's Dr. Williamsen; aren't you going to take it?" Sophia asked. "It could be important."

I scoffed. "I don't know if I can talk to him right now. I fear for what I might say that I'll regret later. I am so angry at him for throwing me under the bus like that, telling them Victor was perfectly capable of going to school when he isn't."

"What did you want him to do? Lie? He's a doctor; he sticks to the facts," Sophia said. "If you're not going to take it, then I will."

"Be my guest. Tell him I'm not here."

Sophia grabbed the phone and spoke to the doctor, telling him I had stepped out for a minute. Then she grew serious, nodded a few times, and said barely anything before she hung up.

The expression on her face made my heart beat faster. "What did he want?"

She took a deep breath. "He wanted to give an update on the boy. The one Maya found."

"Jannik?"

Sophia nodded, biting the inside of her cheek. I didn't care for the look in her eyes. It scared me. Sophia finished her glass, then put it down.

"I think we need something stronger. You got any of that scotch left?"

TWENTY-NINE

Maya immediately noticed that something was off as she came through the front door. The house felt different somehow.

She took off her jacket, and, as she hung it up, she realized what it was.

It feels warm in here. It's not freezing anymore.

Puzzled at this, Maya stepped inside the kitchen where she found her mother and Sophia sitting. They had already finished an entire bottle of wine and moved on to stronger stuff now.

Something was wrong.

"Mom? What's going on? Why does the house suddenly feel so... warm?"

Maya's mom looked up at her. Her eyes were red-rimmed, and she had been crying a lot.

"Mom? What's going on?"

Maya grabbed a chair and sat down. She felt guilty for having been gone so much from home lately, but she couldn't stand the cold, and neither could Alex.

"Mom?"

Her big eyes landed on Maya, and she grabbed her hands in hers.

"You're scaring me, Mom. Just tell me what's going on."

Maya's mom sighed. She looked at their hands and rubbed Maya's in hers. Maya realized that not only wasn't it freezing in the house, but it was also actually getting quite hot, and she was beginning to sweat. That's when it struck her. The cold was gone. That meant her brother wasn't in the house, didn't it?

"Mom? Where's Victor?"

"They... they took him," she said with a sniffle. "They came from the school and told me they were admitting him full-time because he hadn't been to school and he wasn't getting the treatment he needed, and then they had... had gotten a court order, and they took him. Just like that."

"Oh, no, Mom, that's awful. We can't let them do that. We have to get him back. He hates that place."

"I know," Maya's mom said. "But how? They have the law on their side. Morten even helped them take him."

"Morten did?" Maya said, surprised. She had always liked her mother's former boyfriend. It didn't sound like something he'd do unless he were forced.

"He was just doing his job," Sophia said. "We can't blame him for that."

"Of course not. But there is no way we can just sit here and let them get away with taking Victor, Mom. It's not like you to sit there. We need to get a lawyer and fight them."

"That's what I said," Sophia exclaimed. "I think your mom just needs a little time to process all of it. It's a lot right now."

"There's something else," Maya's mom said and lifted her gaze.

"What?"

"The boy. Jannik, the one you found in the shed..." She trailed off, and Maya grew impatient.

"What about him?"

"He died, Maya; oh, sweetie, it's awful. He passed away this morning, and he was... he froze... and..."

Maya let go of her mother's hands. She knew what she was thinking. She was worried that Victor would suffer the same fate. Maya couldn't blame her for thinking like that. Maya had thought about it from time to time as well. She had thought about Jannik and Victor and that girl from the gas station, who had left frost prints on the magazines. Did she have whatever this boy had died from as well? Was it a disease? And if so, did that mean that Victor would die from it too?

THIRTY

Ingrid pulled her bike up the driveway, then put it in the garage. A car was parked on the street outside—a big black SUV—and she wondered if her parents had company. She just hoped they weren't going to stay for dinner. Making polite conversation was the last thing Ingrid was in the mood for.

She didn't quite understand why her parents wanted to have people over on a day like today when she had just revealed her biggest secret to them. She kind of wanted it to be just the three of them, so they could really talk about what she had told them. She knew it had to be hard for them to grasp.

She had left them to go to her meeting with the UFO group but promised they'd talk more once she got back. She had left the house feeling the greatest relief of her entire life. She had always heard the expression of feeling like a huge weight was lifted off her shoulders, but never quite understood it till now. This was exactly how it felt.

She hated keeping secrets from her family because she had always been open with them and told them most things. Even when she started smoking weed and had trouble stopping, she came to them, and they helped her quit her addiction. That was the kind of parents they were—always understanding and compassionate.

Thomas had been very surprised when she told them at the group session how her parents had reacted. He said he hadn't expected them to be so understanding and believed she was very fortunate to have parents like them. Ingrid believed so too.

She closed the garage door, then walked up to the front door and opened it. The handle froze at her touch, and she pulled it back immediately with a small shriek. She hated it when that happened. It wasn't everything that froze when she touched it, but it was happening more and more often these days. She was also getting colder and colder, and it kept her awake at night, the sound of her chattering teeth.

She had thought about asking her mother to take her to see Dr. Williamsen about it, but she was scared. What if he told her she was sick or that she needed to go to the hospital? She didn't feel very ill, except for the body aches and chills. She didn't have a fever. She had taken her temperature this morning, and it was actually pretty low—thirty-four degrees. So, it wasn't some disease that made her like this. At least she didn't believe so.

She was still convinced it had to do with her disappearance and what the aliens did to her. They injected something into her; she was certain of it—something that made her body freeze and everything around her too.

Ingrid took off her coat and hung it up, then walked through the hallway. She was starving but didn't smell any dinner. Maybe they were planning on ordering pizza tonight. Maybe these guests were a surprise visit. It had to be, right?

"Mo-om?"

"In the living room," she answered.

Ingrid didn't like the way her mother's voice sounded. There was something to it that came off as strange, like she was nervous or anxious. Ingrid brushed it off. She was just being paranoid. She smiled from ear to ear as she opened the door to the living room and stepped inside.

"Whose car is that in the..."

Ingrid paused as her eyes fell on the crowd inside her living room, and her eyes locked briefly with her mother's.

"What's going on here? Mom? Who are these people?"

THIRTY-ONE

It felt like he was dreaming—like he was asleep, but he wasn't. It took a while for Tony to realize this, but he was actually awake. His eyelids were still closed, though, but he could hear noises, voices coming from outside his body, and he felt hands touching him.

Where am I? In the hospital? Did something terrible happen to me?

Tony attempted to gather his thoughts. He tried to put the pieces back together and get back to where he was and what he last remembered. He was walking Buddy in the park, yes, and then what? Then there was a bright light, and Buddy ran home, and then...

I was abducted. I was taken again!

Recalling this made Tony's heart beat faster. He realized it had happened just the way it had during the other episodes, yet this time it felt very different. He hadn't woken up somewhere strange, naked, and all alone. But the big question was, where was he? Was he still abducted, and were all those voices he could hear, the small murmuring voices, did they belong to them?

To the aliens?

Oh, my God, I am still with them, aren't I? I am in their spaceship, and they're about to do their experiments. Somehow, their sedative didn't work like it usually does.

Tony did remember kicking and screaming as he felt hands on his body in the park. He remembered seeing a syringe, and he remembered kicking it out of the approaching hand. Maybe they hadn't been able to sedate him properly. Perhaps it was wearing off now, and that was why he was waking up. Did they know?

Does this mean that if I open my eyes, I'll get to see them? Will I see their ugly green faces?

The thought was at once intoxicating and terrifying. To think he could be the only human to have actually seen aliens, to have been face to face with them, was beyond exciting. He would be able to take a mental picture of what they looked like and then make a drawing, maybe have one of those police sketchers who he saw on crime shows come and make a sketch that he could show the world.

He could travel the world and speak, tell people that aliens were real, that he had seen them, and then show people what they looked like. He could write a book—he always wanted to do that—maybe even several books about it and go on TV shows to talk about his encounters.

It was thrilling.

But there was another side to it—one he couldn't ignore. If he did open his eyes, how would they react? Would they be angry and kill him because he had seen them? There had to be a reason they sedated their victims. They didn't want humans to know they existed for a reason, right?

While pondering this, Tony felt something brush against his hand, then some device being attached to his finger. Meanwhile, he kept his eyes closed, debating what to do—if it would be possible for him to open his eyes without them knowing.

Just a small crack. They'll never notice.

Tony took a few seconds to find the courage, then finally let his eyelids open just enough to peek.

What he saw on the other side was so utterly terrifying that it made him shut his eyes again right away, while everything inside of him screamed in panic.

THIRTY-TWO

I served the partly burned chicken for dinner, but neither of the kids ate much. Maya sat with her head bowed and stared at her plate, pushing the potatoes around with her fork. Daniel felt uncomfortable in the heavy atmosphere, and that made him try to hide by turning himself liquid for minutes at a time, then returning to normal. I stared at the puddle on his seat, and seconds later saw him grow out of it again. I knew how much he loved Victor, so it was understandable that he would react in some way.

Meanwhile, I was fighting my tears by stuffing my mouth with food, trying to calm my stomach. It was in knots, and I wanted to scream. We had made it halfway through dinner, and Daniel had been excused, then gone back upstairs, and I could still hear him dripping up the stairs when the doorbell rang.

"I'll go see who it is," I said to Maya, who grabbed her plate, then got up and left. I walked to the door, then pulled it open. Outside stood Morten.

"What do you want?" I asked, already feeling the rage rise inside me. I thought about slamming the door in his face. "You're not exactly popular around here lately."

He sighed and took his police hat between his hands. "I'm sorry, Emma. I want you to know this. I feel awful for what happened today."

I stared at him. Morten wasn't exactly a handsome man, but he had the nicest eyes in the world, and I loved them so dearly. Just like I loved him. But he was the one who had broken up with me to take care of his grown daughter who had tried to kill herself. I couldn't really blame him for his choice, but it still hurt just seeing him, especially after today. It felt like he had betrayed me.

"Morten, listen, I am not in any mood to... I'm having an awful day right now, and I just need to..."

"I just wanted to tell you how sorry I am," he said. "I feel terrible. You know how much I love Victor."

"I do," I said, easing up. "You've always been good to him."

"I just wanted to tell you that," he said and put his hat back on. "Let me know if you need help with anything. Doing what I did today broke my heart. It almost made me want to hand in my badge."

"I know you were just doing your job," I said with a deep sigh. I stared at him, wanting him to grab me in his arms so terribly. I missed feeling his strong hands on me, calming me—what I wouldn't give to have him with me tonight to comfort me.

"All right," Morten said and took a step back. "I just wanted to make sure you were okay."

He paused, and our eyes locked for a few seconds again. That was when I couldn't take it anymore. I couldn't hold back my tears any longer, and they sprang from my eyes. Seeing this, Morten jumped toward me and grabbed me in his arms.

"Oh, God, Emma. I knew this would absolutely devastate you. Let me help you, please."

I looked into his eyes. "You'd do that? You'd help me?"

He nodded. Then he grabbed my face between his hands and kissed me.

THIRTY-THREE

"Mom?"

Ingrid's voice cracked as she looked at her parents. Her mother stood with folded hands, tears springing to her eyes. Her dad stepped forward. He cleared his throat.

"These people are from Fishy Pines," he said.

Ingrid lifted her eyebrows. She could not believe she had heard them right. "Fishy Pines? The loony bin?"

"Ingrid!" her mother exclaimed. "That's not..."

A man in jeans and a sweater that looked handknitted stepped forward and placed a hand on her mother's shoulder to stop her. Ingrid's mom pulled back and let him take over. He was the only one not wearing a long black coat. The rest of the men looked like they had stepped right out of the Matrix films.

"We prefer to call it a mental institution," the man in the knitted sweater said. He held out his hand. "Hi, I'm HP. I'm a doctor at Fishy Pines. Your parents tell us you've been having some issues lately. I am here to help you with that."

Ingrid stared at the man with the soft smile. She looked at the hand stretched out toward her and left him hanging. Then she approached her parents.

"You're... you're admitting me?" she asked.

Her dad reached out his hand to touch her, but Ingrid recoiled. Two of the men in the black coats standing nearest her shivered and buttoned up their jackets.

"Ingrid... you're not well, sweetheart, please understand," her dad said, a deep furrow growing between his eyes. "You just can't see it yourself; most people living with mental illnesses can't. But this has been going on for a little too long. You're out of control. This is for your own sake, sweetie. These people can help you."

Ingrid stared at them. They didn't look much like they came from a hospital. Not even the so-called doctor, that HP guy. His goons looked like they had been in the gestapo or something. Their stern eyes didn't leave her for even a second. She ignored them and faced her parents, hoping to be able to plead some sanity into them, to make them see that they were wrong, to appeal to their common sense.

"But I don't need help. Mom and Dad, I told you what happened, and you said... you said you believed me. You sat right there on that couch and said you believed what I told you. Was that just a lie?"

Her mother teared up now and bit her lip excessively. She reached out her hand to touch Ingrid, but she pulled away.

"Honey. You... you tried to take your own life, right here in front of us. You held a knife to your wrist and everything. How else could we react but to get you the help you need?"

Ingrid gasped. She couldn't believe what she was hearing. "I held it against the skin on my arm, not my wrist. Was that what you got from it? I wanted to show you my blood... because..."

"Honey, you were babbling on about UFOs and being experimented on and whatnot. It's not healthy, you're not well, sweetheart. Please do try to understand. You need help. We're doing this for your sake. We can't give you what you need right now. Fishy Pines can."

Ingrid felt fuming anger. But as she sensed the rage inside of her elevate, she also noticed something else. She felt colder and colder the angrier she got. Frost was falling off from her forehead and upper lip onto the carpet. The area on the carpet where she was standing was getting frozen, shaping a circle of ice around her.

"I don't need help, Mom," she yelled, feeling the rage rise again. It was almost uncontrollable, like now that she had let it loose, it was overpowering her, sending waves of freezing chills through her body. "I need you to be there for me. You said you understood me, you said you believed me, and... was it all just a lie?"

As she spoke, ice crystals shaped in the air in front of her and fell to the ground, where they shattered. All eyes in the room were lingering on her, staring at her in terror. As she moved her head, her hair made a strange tinkling noise, and she realized the tips were frozen.

"Ingrid... please calm down, you're..."

"No! I don't want to calm down, Mom. I am angry because you..."

Her mom stepped back and made eye contact with the doctor. He signaled the men in black coats, and they stepped forward. Two of them grabbed Ingrid by the arms.

"I'm sorry," her mom said and leaned on her husband's shoulder, crying. "I'm so sorry."

The men lifted Ingrid into the air, but as they did, she placed a hand on one man's chest. She felt the power leave her body like a wave of frozen air left her and went straight into his chest. The man let out a loud groan. The area around her hand turned white and frozen, and the man pulled back, his face white as a sheet, holding a hand to his chest while the icy part grew bigger and bigger. He dropped to his knees, gasping for air. The other man let go of Ingrid in fear and pulled away.

Seeing this, Ingrid gasped and stepped back. She stared at

her hand, then down at the man on the floor, his eyes protruding while struggling to breathe.

"Ingrid! What have you done?" her mother said.

"I... I..."

Ingrid looked at her mother, then her father, not knowing what to say or what to do next. The looks on their faces were of utter terror, and she knew everything had changed between them. Nothing would ever be the same again.

Realizing this, she turned on her heel and stormed for the door, leaving frozen footprints on the carpet behind her.

THIRTY-FOUR

I woke up at three a.m. with a deep pounding headache, probably from all the wine and the scotch I had consumed just a few hours earlier with Sophia. I wasn't used to drinking, so even a little made me sick.

But that wasn't what had woken me. The reason was something else or someone. Morten.

I opened my eyes and looked at him. He was putting on his trousers in the dark. I reached over and turned on the lights. He looked at me like he was a child who had stolen biscuits.

"What the heck, Morten? Are you leaving? I thought we... we'd spend the night together."

He smiled, then leaned over and kissed me. He smelled great, just like he had last night when we had made love in my bed. The memory made me smile inside, thinking of how wonderful it had been between us—just like in the old days.

"I'm sorry. But I need to get home."

I stared into his eyes, feeling the disappointment soak through me. "But why? I had hoped we could wake up together and then maybe even eat break—"

He placed a finger on my lips to stop me. "You know I can't do that."

I pulled away. "Because of Jytte?"

He nodded. "You know how it is. I've been gone for too long as it is. If she wakes up and I'm not there, she'll get upset and angry and..."

I bit my lip. "I should have known. Nothing has changed, has it? It's like I'm sleeping with a married man."

He threw out his arms. "What do you want from me? You know my situation. Jytte is doing better, yes, but only because I focus on her now... because I give her the attention she needs."

I exhaled deeply and grabbed a pillow to hug. "I hate that you're such a good guy."

He scoffed. "Yeah, well, sometimes I do too. You know I want to stay the night. You know how badly I want to wake up with you and have breakfast with you and your strange bunch. I love being here at your house more than anywhere in the world. But I'm afraid. You don't know what it's like, living like this. I walk on eggshells around her, watching everything I do or say, constantly terrified that she is going to hurt herself again."

"So, what, that's just it?" I asked, knowing I was being selfish and unreasonable, yet still continuing. "I was vulnerable, and you used that. You took advantage of it, and now you're just leaving. Was that why you came, huh? You pretended it was about me, that you felt bad for me, but it was just so you could get laid."

He put on his shirt, then a sweater. "That's not fair, Emma. You know it just happened. We both wanted it. You did too. You wanted it to happen just as much as I did."

I pouted. "Yeah, well... I thought it would mean more to you. Seeing you leaving in the middle of the night like this makes me feel so... dirty. Like what we did was wrong."

He walked to the door, phone in his hand, checking his messages, then stopped.

"There was nothing wrong with what we did; that's for sure. It felt good."

"Then stay," I said. "Please?"

He sighed. "I can't, Emma. You know I can't."

I threw the pillow at him as he rushed out while I yelled after him, "Fine, then leave. Go home and take care of your daughter. But don't come back here thinking you'll get lucky with me again because it won't happen. Do you hear me?"

I had a feeling he didn't. I heard the front door slam shut, and then his car start in the driveway. I hid my face in a pillow while feeling sorry for myself.

PART III

THIRTY-FIVE

"How do you say, 'It's a lovely day' in Chinese?"

Lisa looked at Camilla. They had arrived at the office early to get ready for the delegation who was coming in today. The Chinese were the first to arrive and had already landed in Copenhagen. Lisa had made sure there was a private plane ready to take them to Fanoe island. They didn't have an airport on Fanoe island, but because the ocean was frozen and the darn icebreakers hadn't been there yet, this was the only way to get them here.

There was a farm down on the south end of the island where the farmer had made one of his fields into a strip to be able to land his own private plane. Lisa had paid him to be able to land her Chinese delegation there as well, and hopefully the North Koreans and the Russians as they were to arrive later in the week.

Farmer Thomasen had asked for a lot of money, and Lisa had complained at first but ended up paying the man what he wanted because he knew very well that he was her only hope. Little did he know that she had planned to expropriate that very part of the island if she was elected again. She wanted to build a real airport, and that was the only place to do it. Thomasen might be laughing now, but she'd make him regret his laughter later on when she took his farm.

"I don't know," Camilla said, while Lisa looked at herself in the mirror, making sure her makeup was impeccable. She smiled at her own reflection. If only the rest of the world took such good care of themselves and aged as well as she did, the world would be a better place or at least prettier.

People always claimed the world was too obsessed with looks while Lisa believed the obsession wasn't nearly enough. There were so many ugly people, and she hated having any of them around her. Take that guy, Officer Bredballe, for instance. He had to take the prize as the least attractive man she had ever seen. Just being close to him made her wince like she feared he was contagious.

"Aren't you supposed to know these things?" Lisa asked, annoyed. "Isn't that what I'm paying you for?"

Camilla wrinkled her nose.

She really shouldn't do that, Lisa thought. If she did it enough, it'd turn to real wrinkles one day that wouldn't go away.

"No. Not really," she said. "You're paying me to get you reelected, and I have to tell you that you're not paying me nearly enough when I think about the conditions you're putting me in, like this meeting with these delegations, for instance. You haven't even told me what they're about. Why are they here? I can't get the press involved if you won't reveal what it is all about."

Camilla almost snorted the last part out, and that made Lisa smile. She walked closer to her, then patted her on her cheek.

"In due time, my dear, in due time. Now, let's meet these people." Lisa shuddered as she said the word. She had always felt repulsed by foreign people in general. But these people served a purpose, one unlike anything any of her predecessors could brag about.

"So, are you not going to tell me why they're here?" Camilla asked with a deep sigh. "How am I supposed to do my work?"

"If all goes well, you won't even have to do anything. I'll be reelected without any effort on your part."

Lisa snorted, annoyed. She turned and looked at her campaign manager. She really hadn't been of much use to her.

"I think this is the beginning of a beautiful friendship. How do you say that in Chinese?" she asked. "You must at least know that much.

"I'll pretend I didn't hear that," Camilla said, as she shook her head at her, then grabbed the door for Lisa so she could step into the lobby, where the Chinese delegation was already waiting.

THIRTY-SIX

I walked the dogs on the beach, mumbling angry words under my breath meant for Morten, then made breakfast for Daniel while Maya slept in. She didn't have to be at the gas station till the afternoon, and I figured she needed the rest. The last couple of days hadn't been easy on her either. She had been shocked after finding Jannik in that shed, and now that he was dead, it had broken her heart.

"I'm gonna go see Victor," I told Daniel, once I had cleaned up after breakfast. Daniel was sitting in his room, reading webtoons on the iPad I had given him. Daniel seemed to be in a better mood today, and I didn't see any part of his body being liquified as he sat there on his bed. He did miss Victor though. I knew that much. His big clear blue eyes looked up at me when I spoke. "At Fishy Pines. I need to make sure that they're taking proper care of him and are monitoring his temperature. I'll tell him you say hello. How about that?"

The young boy nodded, then looked down. "I miss my mom."

I swallowed and thought about Lyn. I hadn't heard from her since last winter. I worried about her.

"She'll be back," I said. "I know she will."

Daniel nodded and returned to his webtoon. I knew he had to be extremely bored, especially now that Victor was no longer here. I would have to figure out what to do with him soon. Me acting as an occasional teacher wasn't really sustainable. The kid needed an education.

I let Brutus in to be with Daniel so he wouldn't be alone while Maya still slept. The big dog sat down by his bed, then stared at me with those light blue eyes. I knew the dog would give his life to save any of the children in my house. He was loyal like that—not like Kenneth, who was mostly a nuisance, albeit a cute one. Lately, he had started eating my underwear, and now I walked around with big holes in them. He had found this technique where he crawled up on my laundry basket, then pulled them out through the holes in the sides. I had renamed him "the little pervert" for that.

I went to my car and got in, then started it up. It coughed a few times due to the freezing temperatures outside, and I shivered before it finally started. My driveway and the roads were icy after another night with temperatures below freezing, which was very unusual for this time of year on our island. Snow fell once again from the heavy gray sky above and made it hard for me to see the road properly.

I couldn't believe how much snow we had gotten already, and it was only November. It was piled up on the sides of the road, and the snowplows couldn't keep up. Usually, we wouldn't have snow till January at the earliest, and if we did, it wouldn't be this much, nor would it be this freezing cold. It had all the weather forecasters puzzled because it was only our island, not the rest of the country, that had been hit this hard.

They both froze to death. Lars, then Jannik. What else did they have in common? One was a grown man, the other a young child. They weren't related as far as I know. Did they know each other? There has to be some connection, doesn't there?

I pondered this while driving up in front of Fishy Pines and parking the car in the lot outside. I sat for a few seconds while looking at the old building in front of me. Behind those walls, my son was being kept prisoner against my will, against his will. And there was nothing I could do about it.

Needless to say, I needed a few minutes to calm myself. I couldn't blow this visit, or it would be the last one I'd get.

THIRTY-SEVEN

What is happening to me?

Ingrid stared at her hands, then turned them in the sparse light. She couldn't believe what she had done, how she had made that man fall to his knees in her parents' living room just by touching him.

She had found a hiding place in the basement of some random house she passed while running away. She had slept on the cold floor, but slept surprisingly well, better than she had for a long time.

As she opened her eyes when the morning light crept in through the small windows under the ceiling, she had forgotten what happened at first. And then she remembered. Devastated, she had recollected the events at her parents' house, how the men had tried to take her, and how she had somehow fought them off by just touching the man's chest. It had terrified her at first but also made her feel powerful beyond anything. To think that she could actually make a grown man fall to his knees like that offered endless possibilities.

But it also scared her because she didn't understand what it was or how it was even possible. She had seen things freeze at her touch, and that had been frightening enough, but this? Would she ever be able to touch anyone again? What if she hurt someone she loved?

I'm turning into freaking Elsa from Frozen!

Now she didn't know what to do. She couldn't contact her parents; they'd just send more of those goons to take her away. And she didn't have any friends she could go to.

There was no one she could trust.

Ingrid looked around, then realized her stomach was growling loudly, demanding to be heard. She had no idea where she was, but if she was in someone's house, there had to be food here somewhere, right?

She walked to the door of the small room, then opened it cautiously. It revealed a hallway of more doors, and she walked through it, then saw a small pantry with tinned food, but no opener anywhere.

She found the stairs and walked up, careful not to make a sound. She found herself in a kitchen, where she spotted a box of cereal on the counter. Hurrying, she ran to it and grabbed it, then hurried back to the stairwell and down the stairs. She rushed into the pantry where she found sodas and bottled waters, then grabbed a couple of each and rushed back to her small room, panting agitatedly as she sat behind the door, waiting to hear if anyone was upstairs—if anyone was coming down after her.

But the house remained quiet.

Then she ate. She stuck her hand inside the cereal box and stuffed her mouth, chewing loudly, then washed it all down with the soda. While she ate, she felt her energy go up just enough for her to think clearer. She felt better than ever, she realized. While she had constantly felt drowsy and like she was about to get sick ever since she was abducted, it was like she was now feeling stronger, like right when she got well after the flu, and she felt so relieved because she had forgotten how life could be, how wonderful it was not to be sick.

Ingrid took another handful of the cereal, then looked at it, wondering why this didn't turn to ice when she touched it. Was it only when she got angry that these things happened? Could it be that there might be a way to control it?

Maybe it wasn't a disease after all that the aliens had given her. Maybe it was a gift, a superpower.

THIRTY-EIGHT

"I'm here to see Victor Frost," I said to the receptionist behind the counter in the lobby. "Can you tell me where I'll find him?"

The woman looked up at me, then down at her papers, pushing her glasses back as they slid down her nose. She flipped a few pages, then looked up at me, her eyes indifferent.

"I'm sorry. Who are you?"

"I'm his mother, Emma Frost. I was told this was the time for visiting hours when I called yesterday."

She drew a deep breath, then glared at her papers briefly before her eyes returned to me so fast it was like she knew she wouldn't find her answer in her documents.

"I'm sorry. That patient isn't allowed to have visitors yet. He's new and needs time to settle before visitors are allowed."

"Excuse me?" I said, already spitting in anger. "You're telling me I can't see my own son."

"That is what I'm saying, yes. It's not unusual. Having visits from parents or other family members can set the patient back and make adaptation to new surroundings slower. I'm sorry."

I looked down at the small woman in the white shirt and

hair tight in a bun on the back of her head. Her upper lip curled as she looked at me, then tried to smile.

"So, when do you expect I can see my son, then?" I asked, fighting to hold my anger back, biting my cheek not to scream.

"Try again next week."

My eyes grew wide, and my heart started to pound like it would explode in my chest.

"Next week? NEXT WEEK?"

I yelled the last part, and the woman exchanged a glance with the security guard standing by the sliding doors. He approached us.

"What's going on here? Ma'am?"

I scoffed. "She won't let me see my son. You can't keep him here without my consent. He's my son!"

The guard sighed, then pulled my arm to make me turn around. "Listen, lady. If the doctors say he can't have visitors, then they have their reasons. They're only trying to do what is best for the child. Now, I have to ask you to leave."

"Leave?" I said, pulling my arm out of his grip. "I'll do no such thing. I demand to see my son. I demand to see Victor now!"

"I'm afraid that isn't possible, ma'am," he said, again grabbing for my arm, but I moved away so he couldn't. I gave him a stern look, letting him know I wasn't someone he'd get rid of that easily. I wasn't going to give up seeing my only son; that's for sure.

"Ma'am. I am going to have to ask you to leave now."

He grabbed my arm, firmly this time, and started to push me toward the door. But I pulled away, then sat down on the floor.

"I am not moving until I'll get to see my son," I said.

The guard exhaled, annoyed. "Ma'am, please. Get up."

I shook my head, holding my arms crossed in front of my chest. "I'm not moving."

"You can't see your son today. Come back next week," he argued.

"Okay, if I can't see my son, then let me see HP. He can tell me why."

The guard looked at the woman behind the counter. "The doctor is busy all day; he's not even coming in today."

"I don't believe you," I said.

The guard sighed again, this time way deeper, then grabbed the radio attached to his shoulder.

"We have a situation in the lobby. Requesting assistance."

Less than three seconds later, two big men came out through the sliding doors. They reached down, grabbed me in their arms, and lifted me in the air like I weighed nothing.

"No!" I yelled while feeling the ground disappear below me. "No, you don't. I want to see my son!"

I screamed and yelled, but it didn't help. They carried me outside, then put me down in the snow. I struggled to get up, then scrambled for the doors again, but the security guard from earlier blocked my way.

"You need to leave before this gets ugly, ma'am," he said.

"But... he's my son. I can't just leave him here and not see him for an entire week. What if he needs me? He's sick; what if he gets worse? Don't you have children?"

"Whether I do or not is of no importance right now. What is important is that you leave before I call the police and have you arrested."

"You'll call the police. You?" I said, scoffing loudly. "You're the ones who have kidnapped my son."

The guard's eyes lingered on me, and he shook his head while his stern eyes eased up a little.

"Please, just leave, ma'am, before a restraining order is put on you. I've seen it before. They won't hesitate to have it done, and then you won't get to see him at all. Leaving now is the smart thing to do, even if it doesn't feel good."

He stared into my eyes to make sure I understood, then turned on his heel and walked inside. The three guards stood behind the door, blocking the entire entrance.

My shoulders slumped, and I felt tears pile up in my eyes as I finally gave up. I turned on my heel and walked away. As I passed the windows, I spotted a little girl and couldn't help stopping to look at her. She was sitting in the window with her nose pressed up against the window. As she breathed on the glass, it froze.

THIRTY-NINE

Maya woke up, then shuddered. She pulled the covers up to warm herself, but it didn't really help. Then she sat up in bed and realized it was past noon. She had slept too late. Maya didn't like sleeping in too late. It made her feel groggy the rest of the day like she never really woke up at all.

Why didn't her mom wake her up earlier?

She rushed into the shower and took a burning hot one but didn't feel like she got warmed up properly.

It had snowed again outside, so she put on jeans and a thick sweater, then went downstairs to get some breakfast. To her surprise, she found the kitchen empty.

"Mom?"

As she looked for her, she found a note on the kitchen counter. *Gone to Fishy Pines to see Victor. Take care of Daniel until I am back.*

Maya sighed and put down the note. She felt awful for her mother and her younger brother. To have to spend his entire day and night at that place had to be killing him. He hated it there.

"Daniel?" she called out. The boy was twelve years old and

perfectly capable of taking care of himself in Maya's opinion, but according to his mother, he needed a sitter. Maya was certain she just feared the people who were after him from Omicon, that they would find out she was hiding him there. She needed eyes on him always.

"Daniel?" she repeated, then walked into the living room where she found him playing Victor's Xbox. He didn't even look at her or hear her, so she returned to the kitchen and grabbed a piece of toast from the table, then buttered it and ate it while washing it down with warm coffee. She held the cup tightly between her hands, yet she couldn't seem to get warm enough. Why was she suddenly so cold?

Maya drank from her cup, then remembered her talk with her mother about Jannik and Victor and how she feared it was some virus causing their temperatures to drop until they died from hypothermia—that it was like they froze from the inside. Now she felt freezing, but Victor was nowhere near.

Had Victor passed it on to her? She had been so careful not to get too close to him.

The girl at the gas station. I touched the magazines after she did. Maybe that's how I got it!

Her pulse quickening, Maya took another sip of the warm coffee and swallowed. Now that the thought had entered her mind, she couldn't stop thinking about it. It could be a virus, couldn't it? It killed that guy on the street, and then Jannik. Maybe they just didn't know it existed yet.

Had a new virus emerged on the island? Or maybe some tourist brought it here, and now it was making its way through the island's inhabitants?

Maya swallowed more coffee, then grabbed another piece of bread and buttered it. There was nothing wrong with her appetite, so that was a good sign. But her hands were so cold, and so was the rest of her body. It was like she was quivering... like she couldn't get the heat back.

Like it came from inside of her.

Just as panic was about to emerge, she saw her mom drive up in the driveway, landing the car in a pile of snow. She got out and walked up to the house with angry steps, and Maya could read the worry on her face.

She couldn't tell her mom anything, she decided as she heard the front door open. She had enough on her plate as it was with Victor. She wouldn't want to burden her with more. Besides, it was probably nothing.

Right?

FORTY

"It's freezing in here again. I thought Victor had left and taken the cold with him?"

Sophia rubbed her hands, then blew on them. She had come over right after I got home. I hadn't noticed the cold, probably because I was so upset; I was fuming, but now that she mentioned it, I did feel it.

"You're right," I said. "It is cold again. That's odd. I don't get it. It went away as soon as Victor left the house, but now it's back. Maybe it wasn't him after all."

"Maybe put some wood in the fireplace and crank up the heat," Sophia said. "Maybe your radiators just broke, I know a guy who can take a look if you like."

"Sure," I said, "that would be great."

The coffeepot was empty, and I assumed it was Maya who had taken the last of it, so I put on a new pot, then went to the living room to put some wood in the fireplace. Daniel was in there, playing Xbox, and it wasn't nearly as cold there as it was in the kitchen. Maybe it was just the radiators.

"Just send me that guy's number, and I'll call him today," I said as I returned to the kitchen. "I think I need it fixed fast with the cold we're having these days."

"It sure is rough out there," Sophia said as the coffee maker spat out the wonderful dark substance. I found some biscuits that were a few days old and put them on the table before pouring each of us a cup. Sophia immediately dug into the biscuits, and I followed.

"So, what's up, why did you text me to come over ASAP?" she asked, crumbs landing on the table below. "They didn't let you see him, did they? At Fishy Pines?"

I shook my head, then dipped my biscuit in the coffee. I found it to be a little dry.

"They have truly kidnapped him. I'm not even allowed to see him," I said, holding back tears. Just thinking about it made me feel so helpless. "Besides, I fear for his safety."

"Why?" she asked.

"He isn't well."

Sophia put her hand on my arm for comfort. "They're doctors, Emma. If he does have a virus, if that is what is causing his body temperature to be so low, then they'll know how to handle it. Right?"

"That's the thing. I am not sure they'll know what to do about it. Dr. Williamsen has no knowledge of any virus causing dangerously low body temperatures. What if it is some new phenomenon? Will they even know what to do to help him? Besides, I don't know if I trust them. Something is going on in that place, and it terrifies me," I said, eating more of my soaked biscuit. "Today, I saw a kid in the window, and as she pressed her nose against the glass, it froze. Just like Victor does."

"Maybe it *is* a virus," Sophia said. "Like we talked about. Maybe the kids are giving it to one another in there. Like that kid from the shed. He was from Fishy Pines as well."

"That's what I'm worried about. He died, remember?" I said.

"Because there was no one to take care of him because he ran away. I'm sure if he had stayed, the doctors could have treated him," Sophia said. "You must give them a little credit."

"But what about Lars?" I asked, leaning back in my chair. "If it is a virus, then how did he get it? He wasn't a patient there, and he doesn't go to the school. Could he have worked there or something?"

That made Sophia laugh. "Ha! Lars? He hasn't worked a day in his life. He was a drunk."

I grabbed another biscuit and dipped it in my coffee. "So, what's their connection? How did he catch this... virus?"

Sophia grinned and sipped her coffee. "Maybe that's what you need to find out. Do a little contact tracing."

FORTY-ONE

"Karin?"

The woman sitting behind the counter at the travel agency was a Kathy Griffin type with brawny slenderness; an open, pleasant face; and flashing brown eyes under her red hair. She looked up at me with a big smile. It didn't hide the sadness beneath it though, which had to do with losing her son recently.

"Emma Frost? What brings you here?"

Her voice was less high-pitched than I remembered.

"Do you have time to talk?" I asked and glanced around me. The agency was empty, which was no surprise. It wasn't exactly tourist season, and with the boats not being able to go to the mainland the past couple of days, there were certainly no tourists coming to the island.

Except for the Chinese delegation, I thought. I had read this morning that they had arrived, and how they had to fly them in and land on Thomasen's fields. Tomorrow, delegations from Russia and North Korea were going to arrive the same way.

"Sure. What's going on?"

She let me in behind the counter and poured me some coffee from her thermos.

"I wanted to talk to you about Lars. I hope you don't mind."

Hearing her son's name made her exhale and her shoulders slump. Her eyes became distant for a few seconds before they returned.

"I'm afraid I don't know much about what happened to him," she said. "They won't tell me anything. He froze to death, but that's all they have said. Are you writing about it in a new book?"

"Maybe. I don't know yet. I just feel like... well, that there is more to the story."

She went quiet, and her eyes landed on the black coffee for a few seconds. "I feel that too," she then said. "They keep telling me that he probably fell asleep, drunk, maybe at the park or in a bush somewhere, and then because of the freezing temperatures we've had lately, he simply froze to death. But the thing is..."

She paused and sipped her coffee, then looked up at me. Her eyes had a terrified, puzzled look to them. She was troubled.

"He was cold long before that day. He would walk around the house, freezing, rubbing himself, massaging his hands and legs. I told him to put more clothes on, but it didn't help. He had those blue lips constantly, and they quivered when he spoke. And it was like... like there was this coldness surrounding him all the time, wherever he went. He brought it with him, and when I was near him..."

"You felt cold," I said, thinking of Victor.

"Yes. Exactly. It got so bad that the entire house became freezing, and I couldn't heat it up. All my plants died, and I had to take my bird to the neighbor's house because I feared it would freeze to death. When Lars touched a surface, like the refrigerator, he'd leave frost behind, or sometimes it would even turn frozen where his fingers had been. His skin felt so cold to the touch."

"Did you take him to a doctor at any point?" I asked.

She shook her head. "No. Lars liked to party, as you might know, and I begged him to stop and see Dr. Williamsen instead, and maybe lay off the booze for a few weeks, but he didn't listen. What can you do when your boy is twenty? You can't force him to listen to you anymore. I wish I had though. I wish I had done more to help him."

I placed a hand on her arm. "You can't blame yourself. I'm sure you did everything you could."

"I just... he was so cold; why was he so freezing cold all the time, Emma? I keep a warm house. He shouldn't have been so cold, should he? What was wrong with him?"

I sipped my coffee and enjoyed the warmth inside the office. The radiators were on max heat while the snow fell slowly outside the windows. "That's what I want to find out. Maybe you can help me. I need to know who Lars was in contact with. Was he close to anyone from Fishy Pines?"

Karin wrinkled her forehead. Her tone was suspicious. "Fishy Pines? The mental institution?"

I nodded.

"I don't think... no; I don't think so, why?"

"Did he have any friends who maybe worked there?"

She thought it over, then shook her head. "Not that I know of. But Lars knew a lot of people. He was a party animal and met so many people at the bars downtown. I guess he could have met someone who worked there."

"But he didn't talk of anyone?" I asked. "Not a new friend or maybe a girlfriend?"

She shook her head, then paused. "There was someone he talked about suddenly—some guy named Thomas. He went to his house a couple of times and hung out with a bunch of others. That's the most recent thing I can recall right now."

"Thomas? Do you have a last name?" I asked.

She shook her head. "I'm afraid not. I didn't listen very carefully because he met a lot of new friends who would soon be gone again. But this was the first guy who invited him to visit him at home and not just be a drinking buddy. That's why I remember, I guess."

"Do you have an address?" I asked.

"I don't. But maybe I can find his number if I go through Lars's phone when I get home. I am sure the number will be there."

I nodded. It wasn't much to go on, but it was at least something.

I left her small office by the harbor, feeling a strange sensation of angst nagging at my stomach. Everything she told me about Lars and how he behaved in the days before his death reminded me of what Victor was like before he was taken away. Karin told me his symptoms began about a week-and-a-half before his death. That didn't leave me much time to save my son.

FORTY-TWO

I drove through town, going home after my visit, fighting my tears, thinking about Victor. I had called the social worker at city hall earlier and left a message telling her we needed to talk about my son, and that I wanted to fight the decision to admit him full-time.

I had also called Michael, my lawyer, but he wasn't available, his assistant said. I felt like people were avoiding me, that no one wanted to face me. Maybe they were right; I was a nuisance, and so be it. I would bother all of them until I got my son back. No one took my Victor away from me. No one.

I was deep in my own thoughts when I came to an intersection by Dagmarsvej, then slowed for a red light. I sniffled and looked out the windscreen while my wipers were fighting to keep the snowflakes at bay. They were coming strongly now, and I had to drive carefully because the roads were icy and slippery.

I sighed as I stared at the red light, waiting for it to change, when something caught my eye. On the other side of the road, also stopped at a red light, was the school bus from Fishy Pines.

I stared at it through my windscreen, leaning forward when the light changed. I didn't drive off yet, as my eyes were fully focused on the bus, my heart pounding in my chest.

Was Victor on that bus?

As it drove past me, I turned to look, and that's when I spotted him. He was sitting in a window seat with his head leaned up against it. I would recognize those curls anywhere. It had to be him.

Someone honked behind me, and I realized I had to move. I pressed the accelerator down intending to continue on my way home. But then something got into me, a thought, a desire to follow the bus, to see where it was going. I turned the car around and slid sideways on the icy road, then got back on track and pressed the accelerator to catch up with it.

I found it on the top of a hill, then followed it closely as it took a right turn. I stayed close behind it, then slowed down slightly so no one would notice I was there. It took another turn and came out on a bigger road leading out of town. Pondering about where it could be going, if the kids were on some sort of field trip, I kept close to the bus until it left town, then took an exit leading up to a big gate where it stopped.

On the gate, a name was engraved. It read, OMICON.

The gate opened slowly, and I watched, my heart beating fast in my chest as the bus drove in and the gate shut behind it. The entrance was packed with cameras, so I decided to move out of their way, fast, so I wouldn't cause suspicion. I drove past the gate and continued down the street until there was a small parking lot. I drove into it, then stopped. I stayed there for a few seconds, heart pounding in my chest, tears spilling onto the steering wheel. I knew a little too well what they did in there.

It's the place where no one hears you scream, Daniel had told me. This was the place Lyn and Skye had run away from. This was where I suspected Skye was being kept.

Why were they taking my son to that awful place? Were they even allowed to do that?

"It'll be over my dead body," I said as I wiped the tears away, then grabbed my phone and called Michael.

FORTY-THREE

"They're asking for proof."

Camilla looked at Lisa. They had been serving the Chinese delegation drinks after dinner. All day, she had tried to tell them about her project, how it worked, and what she believed they could achieve if they bought her product. The Chinese had brought an interpreter with them who had translated everything. They had nodded politely through it all, but Lisa was missing the enthusiasm she had expected. Didn't they know how big this was, what she had her hands on?

It was at least worth billions, if not more. Billions that would benefit both the island and, naturally, also Lisa, who would take a good cut of it for herself. It was, after all, her idea to start this project, and no one at city hall even knew it existed, so they weren't going to ask to get in on the action. She had managed to keep it a secret for years, and it had given her the peace and quiet needed to develop the product properly.

The people working for her at the lab didn't believe it was ready yet, but she did.

"What do you mean proof? Didn't they listen to my presentation?" Lisa asked, annoyed. "Didn't they find it spectacular?"

"They did," Camilla said. "But they're not going to buy anything unless they see proof that it actually works. Those are their words, not mine."

"Well... I can't see why they can't just..." Lisa trailed off. She knew this request was going to be made. She didn't have the proof they needed yet, but it wouldn't be long. Maybe only a matter of a day or two more. She'd have to stall them. Tomorrow, the Russians and the North Koreans would arrive. She'd have to do the presentations over again for their sakes, and then tell them they'd get their proof in a couple of days. It was business, and they'd have to understand that.

"Tell them I'll provide it in two days," she said while feeling uncertain.

"Okay, I'll tell them that," Camilla said, then got up.

Lisa grabbed her phone and walked out into the hallway.

"It's me. Do we have the subject yet?"

"We do, ma'am."

Her eyes grew wide. "You do? Why didn't you tell me?"

He went quiet on the other end. "Well, because we don't know how to make the subject do as told, if you catch my drift."

"I don't. Does it work or doesn't it?" she asked.

"We've been working on this particular subject for quite some time, and it does work; we have seen it in action. The question is how to make it work on command for your presentation, if you know what I mean."

Lisa snorted, annoyed. If they had the subject—if they knew it worked, why couldn't they make it work in front of guests? It was annoying. They had worked on this project for years and years. They were so darn close now, she could almost touch the money.

"Well, work on it then. Don't just blabber with me on the phone. Go, make it work. Now. You have two days to make it work; do you hear me?"

"Yes, ma'am."

Lisa hung up with another snort. She took a couple of deep breaths, calming herself.

All good things will come. In due time, Lisa. In due time.

FORTY-FOUR

They had called an emergency meeting at the UFO group. Ingrid had seen it in the group chat and decided to go, even though she didn't like venturing out of her hiding place. She looked over her shoulder constantly as she rushed down Thomas's street toward his house where she could see the others arriving on bikes and in cars.

She rushed inside and grabbed a cup of coffee, hoping it would bring just a little warmth to her freezing skin. Anything at this point would do.

"Hi, everyone," Thomas started the meeting, and Ingrid sat down in the circle of chairs. "We're gathered here today because one of our members has requested it. Tony?"

Ingrid turned her head to look at Tony, who sat next to Thomas. He didn't look much like himself, though. His lips were blue, the tips of his fingers black, and he was shivering as he spoke.

"It happened again," he said. "Just a few days ago, I was at the park, and the bright light was there again."

A couple of the members shivered. If it was because they were cold or because they knew exactly what would come next and had felt it on their own bodies, Ingrid didn't know. Maybe it was a little of both.

"I was taken again, and Buddy ran away. The dog waited for me when I got back. But..."

Tony slurped his coffee. His breath turned to ice crystals in front of his face as he opened his mouth to speak again. Seeing this, several of the others gasped.

"This time, something else happened," he continued. "Something I don't exactly know how to explain."

"What was it?" a woman named Lina asked.

A look of pain flickered over his face. He leaned forward, holding his cup tightly between both hands.

"I saw... them."

"You what?" Lina asked.

"I saw them. The aliens, the abductors, whatever you call them. I don't know how it happened, or rather I think I might, but I'm not sure. I remember kicking something and then seeing a syringe fly across the asphalt. I don't think they managed to get the sedative properly in me or something. I don't know. I was out, but only for a short while. I woke up right when... when they were about to do their experiments."

Thomas leaned forward on his chair, paler than ever. "You saw them? You actually saw them?"

Tony's eyes met the floor. "Yes."

"What did they look like?" Lina asked, almost breathless with excitement.

Tony lifted his gaze and met Lina's. "That's the odd part. They were humans like you and me. Ordinary human beings. I even think I might have recognized one of them."

A murmur erupted, and Thomas had to stop them. "Wait a minute. You're telling me they looked human?"

"Yes, that is exactly what I'm saying. They were humans. They weren't aliens at all."

"And you recognized one of them?"

"I'm pretty sure, yes. I think I went to school with him. Benjamin. I don't remember his last name. I haven't seen him in twenty-something years. But his eyes... I'd recognize them anywhere."

Another wave of murmurs rushed through the living room until Thomas held up his hand again. "Wait a second. Maybe... I mean come on. Humans? That's ridiculous. We have all been abducted, and we all know it was aliens, am I right?" The group nodded, murmuring still. "I have another theory. Could it be that the aliens simply know so much about us that they're capable of making themselves look like people we know?"

"I think I saw that on a show once," Lina said, "that aliens can do that. They can change their appearance to fit their surroundings and make sure we don't see them. You know like chameleons. That's how they walk the earth and even infiltrate our governments."

"Exactly."

"No," Tony argued, shaking his head. "I'm telling you. They're not aliens; they're humans. And Benjamin is one of them."

"Nonsense," Thomas said, almost laughing at how ridiculous the thought was. "You seem to forget we have seen the bright light too; we've been abducted too. Not recently like you, I admit that, but at some point in our lives. We've been taken and experimented on as well. And I think I speak for all of us when I say that we have no doubt in our minds that we were taken by aliens, am I right? They might have looked human, but that could just be an illusion. Aliens are known to be very good at tricking us humans. They're very devious, those bastards."

The group agreed that Thomas was right. What he said made the most sense, and the talking continued, even though Tony tried to protest. He soon gave up trying to convince them.

Meanwhile, Ingrid stared at Tony, especially at his black fingers and shivering body. Seeing this, he moved closer to her.

"I'm like you now. Ever since they took me, I have been freezing. They did this to me. I saw them inject something into me, through my neck. I felt it sting, and they hooked me up to some sort of machine. I didn't see everything because I drifted in and out of consciousness. But after that, I was like this. When I woke up, I was freezing, and I haven't been able to stop.

"I think they gave me the same virus they gave you. Maybe to see how I would react to it. But I don't think I'm doing very well. I can't sleep; I can't eat. I have this pain in my body constantly—and the shaking that simply won't stop—the chattering teeth, and it is affecting my vision now too. Things become blurry, and I am fre-e-e-zing." He said that last part while his torso trembled heavily.

Ingrid stared at the frostbite on his fingers and wondered how Tony was already in worse shape than her, even though he'd got the virus later. She thought about her encounter with the people from Fishy Pines and how she had been able to stop the man by merely touching his chest. She had sent him to the ground, kneeling. And lately, her symptoms hadn't become worse for some reason. She was freezing still, yes, but she wasn't getting worse, and she certainly wasn't getting frostbitten like Tony.

She remembered reading about that guy who died in the street downtown, that he too had frostbite and had lost several fingers due to it. But her fingers were fine, and so was her skin. She wondered if she should tell him about what had happened in her parents' living room, how she had felt like she was suddenly super strong, but then decided against it.

Instead, she left the meeting early, excusing herself by saying that she had homework to do, then left Thomas's house, running out into the snow. It had gotten dark, and she thought that would be to her advantage. Fanoe was a small island, and people who knew her parents would know she had run away. They might tell if they saw her, and she wanted to stay hidden.

Especially now that she worried she might hurt someone she cared about. She had no way of controlling it, of making sure she didn't freeze someone by touching them.

Should I wear gloves, like Elsa? Or run into the forest? Hide in the mountains somewhere?

Ingrid couldn't help laughing when thinking about her favorite childhood film. How she had always wished she'd been able to freeze stuff the way Elsa did. She had thought it was so cool. Now, she had gotten her wish, but it didn't feel as good as she thought it would. Yet it didn't scare her as much as it did Elsa in the film. She didn't need to build herself a castle of ice to keep people out. But she would like to be able to control it somehow.

Ingrid whistled happily as she walked down the street, then stopped. Around the corner in an alley, two men were carrying something big toward one of the dumpsters. Whatever it was, it was heavy, and they were carrying it like it was... a body.

FORTY-FIVE

Maya's teeth chattered. She rode her bike across the pavement, zigzagging between piles of snow, trying to avoid the worst-hit areas where the plows hadn't removed the snow, or where people hadn't shoveled their sidewalks as they were supposed to. She got stuck in some heavy snow and had to get off the bike to pull it part of the way.

She had been to dinner at Alex's house after work, and Dr. Finnerup had asked a little too much about her brother. He kept digging into details about how cold it had been in the house and if he had frozen things that he touched, stuff like that. Maya had tried to avoid answering but told him that he was now admitted full-time at Fishy Pines because he was skipping too much of his education. It didn't come as a surprise to Dr. Finnerup, and Maya wondered if he already knew.

She hadn't enjoyed dinner much and told Alex she wasn't well and left right after. She had been cold at his house, but not as bad as she had earlier in the day, and she wondered if she might be getting better. Yet now she was freezing again, her fingers hurting as she pulled the bike. Finally, she made it downtown where the snow had been removed, and she got back up on her bike and was about to step on the pedals when a noise made her stop.

It was coming from an alley next to her, and as she looked to see what it was, she saw a black SUV parked there. Two men dressed in dark clothes were doing something, and as she walked closer, she realized they were fighting with someone.

Maya squinted her eyes to see better. She couldn't believe she had seen it right.

Was the one they were fighting a young girl?

It can't be!

But it was. Maya took another step closer as she saw one man grab the girl and lift her. The girl squealed, and Maya let go of her bike. She reached inside her pocket to grab her phone, but as she pulled it out, she saw something she hadn't seen coming. The girl roared loudly, then placed a hand on the man's face, and immediately, he froze. His face froze to ice, and it didn't stop there. It spread down his neck, and soon his entire body became stiff as a board. The girl fell in the snow, and the man tipped forward, face-first into the snow. Seeing this, the other man stood for a few seconds, staring at the girl, then pulled a gun on her. With a quivering voice, he yelled. "Come any closer, and I'll shoot!"

The girl stood completely still at first. Then she burst into laughter. She took a step closer to him, then another one, and now Maya recognized her. It was the girl from the gas station. The one who had given her the virus. Why was she here fighting those men?

The girl took another step toward the man with the gun, and as she did, he panicked. He turned around and ran, screaming down the alley, then jumped into his car and took off, almost knocking Maya over as he passed her, splashing snow on her.

She looked after the SUV as it disappeared, then back at the girl who was now bent over something on the ground, a black plastic bag. Maya walked closer, slowly, and now the girl saw her. Frightened at first, Maya took a step back, but the girl tried to smile, and her eyes weren't threatening.

They were kind. And a little desperate.

"Help me with this, will you?"

"O-okay," Maya said.

"They were trying to dump it here," the girl said. "In those dumpsters."

Maya walked up to the girl and helped her open the bag. As they did this, Maya's heart started to bounce in her chest. First, she saw the feet, then the legs, and as the small body of a young girl was unraveled, she turned around and threw up in the snow.

FORTY-SIX

I came as soon as Maya called me. I drove through the thick snow that kept falling in an endless stream, then parked in the alley. I walked up to Maya, who threw herself in my arms.

"Oh, Mom, it's awful."

I stared at the body on the ground. A young child, a girl, and not far from her, a man wearing all black, completely frozen, was headfirst in the snow.

"Tell me what happened," I said.

Maya sobbed, then wiped her nose. "I was... and then I came back and that's and then... oh, my God, Mom, the girl, she was... she was... she put her hand and then this guy, and the other pulled a gun—"

"Hold on. Hold on, sweetie. You need to slow down a little. You're not making much sense here. Try again." I grabbed her by the shoulders and looked into her eyes. It seemed to calm her a little. "There you go. Try again, sweetie. Slowly."

She took a ragged breath, then whimpered slightly before she opened her mouth.

"I was on my way home from Alex's place when I heard noises coming from the alley. I stopped, and I saw this girl. She was fighting with these men, and then she... she froze..." Maya turned around and pointed at the man in the snow. "Him."

"She froze him?"

"Yes. She put her hand on his face and held it there until he was completely frozen. He then fell, and the other guy tried to shoot her, but ran off instead, drove away in a black SUV."

"And the girl? Where is she now?"

"She ran," Maya said. "She said she couldn't be here when the police came. I helped her unwrap the body in the bag, and when we saw her, she knew she had to leave."

"Did she say why?" I asked. "Why was she in a hurry to get away?"

Maya shook her head. "She didn't say. But I sensed that she was scared. I have seen her before, though. I know who she is. I think her name is Ingrid. She comes to the gas station or... she used to. I think she has whatever it is Victor has because the things she touched at the gas station froze. I remember thinking Victor might have the same virus as her."

Maya paused. She looked at the girl on the ground, then up at me. "What do you think happened to her? Why did they try to get rid of her?"

I walked closer to the young girl, then realized with great dread where I had seen her before. She was the girl who had been in the window at Fishy Pines, pressing her nose against the glass.

"Oh, dear Lord," I said and clasped my mouth.

"What?"

"She's from Fishy Pines," I said. "I've seen her there."

"From the place that has taken Victor?"

I nodded.

"D-do... you think she got the virus there? Is it contagious?"

I smiled and kissed my daughter on the forehead, trying to calm her. I could tell she was getting too agitated.

"You're cold, sweetie. Let's get you into the car while we

wait for Morten and his team to arrive. I called him on my way here."

I put my arm around her shoulder while we walked back to my car. I looked down at the frozen guy with an exhale. I had seen him before. He was one of the goons who had been there on the day they took Victor.

FORTY-SEVEN

"Not another one!"

Morten rubbed his scalp under the hat while shaking his head in anguish. We were standing bent over the young girl's dead body. Morten had been dealing with a domestic dispute at the other end of town when we called, and it took him about ten minutes before he got there. Maya and I had both come out of the car to show Morten. I suggested that Maya stay in the car, that I'd come to get her once Morten needed her statement. Yet she insisted on coming with me.

"I'm afraid so. Looks like she has frostbite on her fingers and neck," I said. "Just like Lars and Jannik."

Morten was on the verge of tears. I could see in his eyes that he was fighting to stay composed.

"Why does this keep happening? What the heck is going on here on my island, Emma?"

"I wish I knew," I said with a deep exhale. The poor girl couldn't be more than twelve or thirteen. Same age as my Victor.

"Who is she?" he asked, kneeling next to her.

"We don't know," I said. "But, I do know she is from Fishy Pines."

Morten lifted his gaze and met my eyes. "Really?"

"Yes. The frozen guy over there and his buddy were trying to dump her in the dumpster over there when Maya stopped by. Actually, there was someone else here... a girl, and she stopped them from getting rid of the body."

Morten walked to the frozen goon in the snow, then looked down at him. "What happened to him? He's frozen too."

I swallowed. This wasn't easy to explain without sounding like I belonged at Fishy Pines myself.

"We don't really know," I said and exchanged a glance with Maya. We had talked about what to say, but had not come up with a believable story, so we had decided to stick to the truth. It was up to Morten if he believed us or not.

"We think... that the girl froze him. I know it sounds odd, Morten, but Maya watched it happen. She was as shocked as you look right now, but..."

"She touched him," Maya took over. "And then he froze immediately. They were trying to grab her. She told me it was because she had seen them try to dump the body. She was acting in self-defense."

Morten stared at both of us in disbelief, then shook his head. "Wait a minute here. Time out. Back up for just a second. There was someone else here?"

"Yes. A girl a little younger than Maya."

"She was the one who disappeared from the park a few weeks ago, then turned up on the beach naked," Maya said.

Morten stared at Maya, holding his hand up, then lowering it, a confused look in his eyes. No, it was more than that. He was baffled, unable to make sense of it all, his eyes growing distant while trying to put the pieces together, but coming up short, just like the rest of us.

Morten wrinkled his forehead and returned to us. His tone was sharply questioning.

"Ingrid?"

Maya nodded. "Yes, she ran before you got here. Said she didn't dare to be here when the cops came or something like that."

"Her parents did report her missing a few days ago after she ran away from home. Do you have any idea where she might be, Maya? It's important that we find her."

She shook her head, then shuddered in the cold. I put my arm around her to warm her. She felt frozen. She had been outside for a very long time. I had to get her home as soon as possible.

"Morten, let me cut to the chase here. The bottom line is this. These guys are from Fishy Pines," I said. "That one over there... if you look closely at him, you'll recognize him from the day they took Victor. They were trying to get rid of a little girl's dead body. Instead of focusing on Ingrid, you need to look closer at that place, start an investigation into what is going on up there. Something is not right, and you know it as well as I do. You're the only one who can stop them before more kids turn up dead. Now, if you'll excuse me, I have to get my daughter home. If you need anything else, you know where to find us."

Morten stood back, mouth gaping, eyes following us as we walked to the car, got Maya's bike strapped to the back, and took off.

FORTY-EIGHT

"There you go."

Maya's mom handed her a cup of hot chocolate. She had put wood in the fireplace and wrapped a blanket around Maya on the couch in the living room, trying to warm her up.

"Are you feeling better?" her mother asked and removed a lock of hair from her face. "You're getting some color in your cheeks again. That's good."

"I am feeling a little better," Maya said, mostly to calm her mother so she wouldn't worry so much. Maya hated seeing that expression of concern on her mother's face, especially when her upper lip pulled up into a small curl. That usually meant she was broken with worry on the inside but trying hard to hide it from her children.

"This is nice."

Maya's mom smiled and sighed with relief. She grabbed her own cup of hot chocolate and wrapped her feet in a blanket too. They sat still for a few minutes, both looking into the fire, while things settled on the inside.

Maya tried to push it back, but still, the fear kept creeping back in her mind. After seeing that girl in the snow, she felt terrified. Had the virus killed her? Maya felt more and more convinced that she too had gotten the virus and that soon it was going to be her lying there, completely stiff.

But Ingrid hasn't died. Neither has Victor. Maybe it isn't everyone who dies from this.

The thought calmed her slightly, and she sipped her hot chocolate, then shivered again as cold ran down her spine.

"Are you still cold?" her mom asked, then rubbed her shoulders. "It is quite cold in here. I don't understand it because I've cranked the heat up again, and we have the fireplace running. That usually heats the house fast."

Her mother stopped talking when she spotted her plants in the windowsill. She rose to her feet and looked at them closer.

"They're dying!" she exclaimed. "All my beautiful plants are dying from this freaking cold!" She turned to look at Maya. "I thought it was because of Victor that the house was constantly so cold. I was so sure that was why, and it did go away when he left, but now it's back. I don't get it. I even had a guy check everything out, and he couldn't find anything wrong."

It's me, Mom. I think it's because of me. I got the virus, and I am causing everything to freeze.

Maya thought about Ingrid and how sick she had looked. Her lips had been purple, almost blue, her breathing ragged, and her eyes glassy. And how pale she was. It was almost like her skin was made from ice that could crack at any second. Just being close to her was like standing inside a freezer. It almost hurt Maya's skin. And what she did to that guy. Just by her touch. She didn't even have a very big hand.

It was beyond terrifying. Maya didn't want to end up like that.

"Do you think what Victor has is contagious?" she asked.

Her mom exhaled, then shrugged. "I don't know, sweetie.

Try not to think about it. Get some rest while I prepare dinner, okay?"

Her mom finished her chocolate, leaned over and kissed her forehead, then disappeared into the kitchen, leaving Maya rattling her teeth in both fear and cold.

FORTY-NINE

Sophia came over after dinner. We sat in the kitchen as Maya was still in the living room. She seemed to have calmed down a little and was watching YouTube videos on her phone. I was worried about her. Seeing two dead children in less than two weeks had to be rough on her. She seemed like she was carrying the weight of the world on her shoulders, and I wondered what was going on inside her—whether she would be all right. I wanted her to put more words on her recent experiences, but she didn't want to talk anymore, she told me, brushing me off.

I told Sophia everything that had happened over a glass of white. I told her about seeing the school bus drive into Omicon, and then the finding of the young girl from Fishy Pines.

"Ugh, that awful place," Sophia said, shuddering. "I can't stand the thought that Victor is out there right now."

"That makes two of us," I said with a scoff. "But what can I do? I talked to my lawyer today, and he says there really isn't much we can do right now. I have to show them that I am cooperating and not trying to sabotage their treatment if I want to see him. They have every right to admit him because the doctors believe it is necessary."

I was drinking my wine when my phone vibrated on the counter. I picked it up. It was Morten, much to my surprise.

"I need to ask you a question," he said, sounding awfully professional.

"Okay?"

"Are you certain the girl was from Fishy Pines?"

"Absolutely. I saw her there; she was sitting in the window. She has a birthmark on the side of her cheek that I recognized. Why?"

Morten went quiet for a few seconds. "They say they don't know her. She doesn't exist in their records. She doesn't belong to any school here on the island either, and no one reported her missing. I can't figure out who she is."

"Excuse me?"

He exhaled on the other end. It didn't sound good and made me kind of anxious.

"I don't know what to do. I can't start an investigation into them if the girl didn't come from Fishy Pines."

"Jannik did too, and they admitted that."

"But they also said he ran away and froze to death in the shed. There is nothing to indicate a crime, Emma."

"But this girl was already dead, and they were definitely getting rid of her body," I said.

"Did you see them do it?"

"No... but..."

"You only know it to be true because Maya saw it. You're not even a firsthand witness, and actually, neither is Maya. You're basing it all on the account of what Ingrid told her, and we can't even find her. Can you see how my work is getting hard here, Emma?"

I leaned back in the chair. "I see that."

"I do want to believe you and Maya more than anything, you know this, but right now, I can't really start an investigation based on what I know. All I have to do is to find out who the heck this girl is and where she is from. The autopsy will show what killed her, but if she froze to death like the others, I can't really claim a crime has been committed."

"But what about the guy? You know he was from Fishy Pines, right?"

"I can't prove it. I found his ex-wife. She lives up north and told us he took a job for a private security company. But the company tells us they can't provide information about their employees or their clients without me having a warrant. And I still can't prove that he was trying to get rid of the body if Ingrid won't come forward and tell us. That means I won't be able to get that warrant. There are just a lot of closed doors here. And are you absolutely sure Maya doesn't know where she went?"

I stared at the darkness behind the windows outside, then shuddered with cold. My house felt almost colder than outside these days, and I couldn't for the life of me figure out why.

"I'm afraid not. I'll ask her again though and let you know if she says anything useful. We need to find her at all costs. It can't be that easy to hide on our small island, can it?"

"Apparently, it is," he said. "She's been in hiding for several days, and then she just appeared as if out of nowhere. Listen, I gotta go. Talk to you later, okay?"

"Okay. Love you."

I hung up, then clasped my mouth. I glared at Sophia, who was grinning from ear to ear.

"Did I just say what I thought I did?"

"You did. You totally did."

"I can't believe myself. I actually told Morten I loved him. It was just out of old habit."

"No, it was not. You still love him. We all know you do. Heck, he loves you too. I wish you two could just figure that out and get back to normal. It's sickening to look at."

I put the phone down, thinking maybe he didn't hear it. I was still angry at him for using my vulnerability to sleep with me. But I had to admit I was glad to have seen him today, and I kind of liked being involved in his investigation. It made me feel close to him again, like we were sharing a secret. I missed being close to him like that, sharing things.

Maybe one day.

I sat down and poured myself another glass. Sophia smiled at me. "So, what do you do next?"

"I... I gotta get Victor out of that place before he is the next to be found dead in some weird dumpster or a shed. There must be a way to get him back. I had hoped that if Morten opened an investigation, then maybe they'd shut the place down, but that's not gonna happen anytime soon. I can't wait for them to connect the girl to Fishy Pines. I can look for that girl, Ingrid, but it might take a long time before she's found. I'm not sure I can wait that long."

"So, what are you going to do?"

I stared out the window again at the snowflakes falling in the light from the streetlamps. The sidewalk was already covered in another thick layer that would have to be shoveled in the morning. The city snowplows would be out early in the morning. Our mayor had promised to keep the roads clear so people could get to work, and the kids get to school. There weren't enough plows, so they'd just have to work all night, she had said earlier in the day on local TV while she also spoke about her successful meeting with the Chinese delegation earlier in the day.

"Emma?"

I turned to face Sophia. "Well, if the police can't shut them down, then I'll just have to go to the higher powers," I said.

"What? Like God?"

I shook my head. "No, but pretty darn close. At least she likes to think so."

FIFTY

"You're telling me that this girl froze a man's heart simply by touching his chest?"

Lisa stared at Dr. Finnerup, who was standing across the room. He was darkly handsome with high cheekbones and thick black eyebrows. His dark brown hair had touches of gray. He was wearing a navy-blue pinstriped suit. It was still early in the morning when he came to her office at city hall, and his breath reeked of coffee even though she was standing at least two meters away.

He nodded. "Yes. They don't know if he'll make it. His heart cut out immediately, and they're keeping him alive artificially."

Finnerup placed a couple of photos on her desk, and Lisa looked at the man attached to tubes in a hospital bed. She felt something stir inside of her, something big, something almost arousing and overpowering.

This is it. This is what I've been waiting for!

"I don't care about his condition; I care about the girl. She's one of them. Are you certain of that?"

He nodded again. "Yes. She was abducted a couple of

weeks ago. Her parents called for help, and she was supposed to have been admitted to Fishy Pines a few days ago, but she escaped."

Lisa's eyes went wide as she stared at the man in the suit. Dr. Finnerup was always so impeccably dressed. Classy. There ought to be more like him, she believed. She hated all those jeans and sweater-wearing hipster types. Especially among the millennials. That awful generation of latte-drinking youngsters who believed at thirty they were still too young to settle down and have a family. She had more than once showed them they needed to up their game to make it in this world. As soon as she had become mayor, she had fired anyone who didn't dress properly.

"And did she really freeze this man's heart?" Lisa asked, making sure she didn't hear him wrong. "Just by touching him?"

"Yes."

She sat down in her office chair and looked at the photos, almost overwhelmed to tears. For so long, she had worked on getting to this point. So long.

"That is interesting, so very interesting."

"There is more," Finnerup said.

She looked up at him, eyes protruding with eagerness to hear what else he had to say.

"Really?"

He nodded. "Last night, two of our men came across her again, and she... well, I only know what the one who escaped told us, but he said that she... she touched one of our guards on the head, and immediately he froze to ice. He was dead instantaneously."

Lisa rose from her chair and pushed it back across the floor. "Oooh. She killed him with just one touch. She must be growing stronger then."

"That's what we believe, yes."

"And the girl. Where is she now? Tell me we have her," Lisa said.

Dr. Finnerup's lips grew narrow. His frown made deep crease lines in his forehead and around his eyes.

"You don't have her. How is that possible?"

"She escaped. Twice. She's very powerful, ma'am."

"You!" Lisa spat. "I have the Chinese here, and the Russians and the North Koreans will arrive tomorrow. What do you want me to tell them, huh? That we have what they're looking for, but we can't show it to them?"

"N-no. Of course not."

Lisa slammed her fist onto her desk in anger. "Then find her! Find me that girl now!"

Dr. Finnerup recoiled in fear, then nodded. "Yes, ma'am."

A knock on the door made her look. "Yes?"

It was her assistant, Louise, who peeked inside. Yet another annoying Millennial who couldn't get her life together and who was constantly offended over this and that. Who raised these kids? Had all parents had a collective meltdown?

Not everyone gets a trophy in life!

"What?" Lisa hissed.

Louise looked terrified at her. "Th-there's someone here to see you."

Lisa sat down with a snort. "We were done here anyway. Who is it?"

FIFTY-ONE

They didn't believe him. Tony couldn't get over the fact that his group had discarded his story of what he had seen during his last abduction, and how they might not be from outer space after all. It was the first time his group hadn't believed him. It was the first time he felt utterly rejected by them.

He would never have thought that would happen. By anyone else in the world, yes, but not by them. And now Tony felt like he was all alone in the world.

The microwave in the kitchen dinged, and he took out his shepherd's pie dinner, then walked to the living room where he would eat in front of the TV. Buddy was lying on the couch, sleeping. The dog barely reacted when Tony came into the room and sat down, which worried Tony because the dog would usually always sit by his chair when Tony ate, and they'd share the food. But today, Buddy didn't even seem interested in the food. He just lay there, sleeping.

"Not hungry, huh, Buddy?"

Tony looked at the dog, then grabbed the remote to turn on the TV. He shivered as he touched the plastic, and it froze, then cracked. Tony put it down with a gasp. The ice crystals from his breath hung in the air in front of him, then fell to the carpet below. Tony stared at the food, then realized he wasn't hungry either.

His body was aching and throbbing. It felt like someone had poured lava over his face, then stabbed him with a thousand knives. The freezing had stiffened his lungs, and it was painful to breathe. It felt like he was breathing in knives and exhaling fire. His vision turned blurry from time to time, and often he thought the ground was moving when it wasn't.

Tony closed his eyes and rubbed them. It was like even they were frozen. When he opened them again, he felt almost like he was at sea. The entire room was spinning out of control, and Tony clutched the armrests so he wouldn't get dizzy, but it didn't help.

Confusion seemed to overwhelm him as he tried desperately to recall what he was doing and why he was sitting there. He got up on his feet and glanced around him, the wobbly ground threatening to swallow him.

What is this place? What am I doing here?

"It's your own house, dummy," he reminded himself as he realized it. Then another wave of confusion and hopelessness overwhelmed him.

"I need to get out of here," he mumbled, then tried to walk, but stumbled over his own feet and landed face-first on the carpet, tipping over the tray with the shepherd's pie on the table next to his chair. The food came down, along with all the utensils, and it woke up the dog, who opened his eyes and stared tiredly at Tony.

"I don't know what I'm doing," he wept, then sat up and brushed off the mashed potatoes that had landed on his trousers. "I am so cold it hurts! Please. Someone, help me!"

Tony got to his feet by pulling himself up, holding on to the side of the chair. The dog dozed off again. Tony could see Buddy's breath as it met the cold air.

Why is it so darn cold everywhere?

Tony felt a sharp pain in his arm and pulled up his sleeve to look at it. His veins had turned black, and his arm was stiff as a board. Soon, it was covered in white frost that made the skin turn black beneath it, then crumble and fall off. The black remains drizzled onto the carpet below.

"I need help," Tony mumbled, as he held on to the chair in order not to fall. "I need to call for help."

He spotted his phone on the coffee table in front of him, then reached over to grab it. He tapped on the screen frantically. But the more he touched it, the more it froze to ice. Ice crystals grew until they covered the screen, and it cracked between his hands.

"No!" he exclaimed, trying to get it to work again, but when it wouldn't, he threw it across the room.

"I gotta get out of here. I gotta find help."

He staggered toward the front door while the world spun, and it felt like he was riding a roller coaster. He fell to his knees, and that was when his right leg became stiff, and he could no longer move it. Dragging it behind him, holding out the only arm he could move, he reached for the door handle and grabbed it. But as he did, the handle froze, and so did Tony. Hand still on the knob, he realized he could no longer move any parts of his body.

FIFTY-TWO

Maya's stomach grumbled so loudly it was embarrassing. She was standing behind the counter at the gas station, taking care of a customer when she felt the nagging hunger. She regretted not having eaten any breakfast this morning, but she hadn't been able to find her usual cereal, and there was nothing else she was in the mood for. Her mom had left early and not woken Maya in time, so she had been late for work, which wasn't exactly popular with her boss, who already hated her. At least she wasn't as cold here as she was at home, and that made her think that maybe she was getting better. Maybe she was actually beating this strange virus.

"Do you remember that girl who was in the other day?" she asked her coworker, Angela, as her customer left.

"Which one?" Angela asked, while tapping on the register and scanning some chips and a pack of gum for a customer. She told him the price, and the guy handed her the money.

"The one you said had disappeared and then showed up again on the beach and that everyone was talking about her?"

Angela nodded and gave the customer his change, then closed the register. "Sure. Ingrid? What about her?"

"Do you know her?" Maya asked. "I mean apart from the rumors and seeing her here."

"As a matter of fact, I do," Angela said.

The customer left, and the shop was empty for a few minutes.

Someone drove up outside and began to fill their tank with gas.

"She lives only two blocks down from me, but you're not going to find her there if you're looking," she said. "She's gone missing. The story goes that her parents tried to admit her to the mental place, you know, Fishy Pines."

Maya already knew this but played along. "Why?"

Angela approached Maya, then continued with a low voice as a new customer entered the shop and started to look at sodas in the fridge. They both knew this guy, as he was a regular who came in every day to get his beers, but he'd start by looking at sodas to seem less like a drunk. As if he were fooling anyone.

"Something about her believing she was abducted by aliens and stuff. Anyway, her parents tried to admit her, but she escaped, and now they're searching for her."

"Do you know where she might be hiding?" Maya asked while the customer now moved from the refrigerated case with sodas to the one containing beer. He'd soon grab a six-pack, then walk up to the counter with a sheepish look on his face, as usual.

"No. How am I supposed to know?" Angela said with a grin.

Maya shrugged. "I don't know. Maybe you heard something."

The guy brought his beer to the counter and avoided eye contact as he placed a porn magazine next to them. Angela scanned both, took his money, then wished him a good day, and he was on his way, rushing out with his goods hidden in a bag.

Angela turned to face Maya. "Why are you asking about her?"

"I was just... curious."

She could tell Angela didn't believe her and turned to look away. She had promised her mom to try to find Ingrid but didn't know any of her friends on the island. She knew she was part of this Wiccan group, but she didn't really want to have to talk to them.

"But I might know something that can help," Angela said.

"What's that?"

"I know that Ingrid started going to the local UFO group. You ever heard about that?"

Maya blinked. She had been to the group once back when she was with Samuel, while they were trying to figure out what had happened to their friend Asgar. But she couldn't tell Angela that. She'd get suspicious. The last thing Maya needed right now was for the town's gossip girl to start talking about her.

"I... I haven't, no."

Angela leaned closer and spoke with a low, secretive, yet mocking voice. "Well, it's this group where they meet and talk about being abducted and stuff—by aliens. They're all a bunch of nutcases, just like Ingrid. I guess she fit right in."

Angela started laughing while Maya remembered the meeting she had been to with Samuel about a year ago. She had believed they were all a little nuts too, but with what she had seen and gone through the past year, she was beginning to think that maybe they weren't so crazy after all.

FIFTY-THREE

"Emma Frost! To what do I owe the honor?"

I walked into the mayor's office, feeling all kinds of conflicted. I didn't care much for this strange woman who was the political leader of our island. I had more than once crossed paths with this woman, and she rubbed me the wrong way. To be honest, I thought she was insane. But now I needed her help. I needed to appeal to her decent side, her sensible side. If she had one.

Needless to say, I had my doubts, and being greeted by her didn't exactly make me feel more comfortable. She had these manic eyes and a high voice that made me uneasy.

Yet I managed to smile. Lisa pointed at a chair across from her desk, and I sat down.

"Was that Dr. Finnerup I saw leaving?" I asked. I had been quite surprised to see Daniel and Alex's father walk out of the door just as I arrived, and it had added considerably to my nervousness.

Lisa stiffened for a second, then smiled again. "Yes. Do you two know each other?"

"I know his son. He dates my daughter. He works for Omicon, right? He's the CEO there?" I asked.

Lisa folded her hands across the desk. "Yes, you're right."

I stared at her, wondering if she would elaborate in any way, why the CEO of a private company was holding a private meeting with the mayor, but she didn't. I guess she felt it was none of my business. She seemed annoyed that I was asking, so I let it be. The last thing I wanted was to get on her bad side at this moment. I needed her to want to help me.

"What can I do for you, Emma? I am quite busy, as you must know."

"Ah, yes, the election is coming up. I'll make it brief."

"Please do," Lisa said and looked at her watch.

"I am here because of my son, Victor. He's not quite like other children and has a type of Asperger's, but the doctors have never really been able to diagnose him properly."

Lisa already looked like I was losing her—like she couldn't care less, so I decided to skip to the point.

"Anyway, I am here because they have taken him away from me, and they won't even let me see him."

Now, I had her attention. She had two children of her own whom she felt very protective of. I hoped to appeal to the mother in her.

"Who took him, Emma? I'm not getting it here."

"Fishy Pines."

"Well then, that's probably because the doctors there felt like it was what was best for him," she said.

"But something is wrong in that place," I said, sensing I was losing her attention. Fishy Pines was run by the city, so this was her responsibility. I needed her to be reminded of that.

She smiled. "Like what?"

"Children dying," I said, then showed her a newspaper article on my phone with a picture of Jannik. "This boy came from there. He was found in a shed, nearly frozen, and he died a few days later. I'm sure you've heard about it. He was their responsibility. That makes him your responsibility."

"He ran away, Emma, and froze to death in a shed. It's a tragedy, yes, but no one is to blame. We have upped the security in the place so that it won't happen again. It's really all we can do."

"Then what about her?" I asked and showed her a picture of the girl from the alley that I had taken the day we found her, thinking I would need it someday.

Lisa looked at it, her eyes indifferent. "I don't know who that is. Listen... I..."

"She was also in their care," I said. "They refuse to acknowledge it, and she isn't in their records, but I saw her there when trying to visit my son. She was sitting in the window. And now she's dead. Two dead children within just a few weeks. How do you explain that?"

"How do you know all this, and how do you have that picture?" Lisa asked. Of course, she was trying to make it about me. It was typical of her.

"That's not important here. What does matter is that I know she froze to death just like the boy, and I know for a fact that two guys from Fishy Pines tried to dump her body downtown. I'm telling you something is wrong in that place. And now that we're at it, I have to say that you need to be careful about being seen with Omicon. I sure hope this town is not supporting them in any way. I know that they've taken some of the kids from Fishy Pines to Omicon, and I think that they're doing terrible things to them there. One child told me it's the place where no one hears you scream."

Lisa had stopped smiling, and I didn't even notice until now. She was staring at me, her manic protruding eyes fixated on my face. She was biting the insides of her cheeks.

I glared back at her, my heart pounding, wondering what

she was going to say. I knew how crazy I must have sounded. Yet I felt like I had to put it all out there.

Lisa burst into loud, roaring laughter.

"Oh, my, Emma, what stories you can come up with. Good thing you're the writer, and I'm not. Is this the storyline for a new book?"

I slammed my hand onto her desk. "It's not fiction. Fishy Pines is involved with illegal activities, and it is your responsibility as the mayor. If you don't look into it, and hopefully close the place down, then I will write to every newspaper on this island and let them know what's going on and that you're collaborating with these people. I hardly think you'll be reelected after that scandal is released."

"Okay, okay," Lisa said, lifting her hand to stop me. "You seem to be serious about this. All right. You've made your case. I'll take a closer look at their activities. If anything is found to be illegal or even questionable, then I'll close it down. Of course, I will. But you better not be making these accusations just to get your son back."

"That is not the only reason, and you know it."

I rose to my feet with an annoyed snort. I walked to the door when she stopped me. She suddenly sounded sincere.

"I'll get to the bottom of this, Emma. Don't worry. I promise you I'll do my best to figure out what is going on, okay? I didn't know that two kids had died; I had only been told about the first one. The last thing we want is for any kids to suffer. It's something I feel very strongly about."

I felt my shoulders come down with relief, and my body relaxed slightly. She sounded like she really meant it.

"Thank you," I said. "You're not so bad after all. Maybe I'll even vote for you at the election this time."

That made Lisa laugh again. I could still hear the sound of her laughter as I closed the door, smiled at the assistant, then left.

FIFTY-FOUR

Lisa was tapping restlessly with her long nails against the polished wooden desk. The door had closed behind Emma Frost, and she had left. Lisa had laughed at Emma's joke, but now she had stopped. It wasn't that funny anyway. Nothing about Emma's visit had been amusing. On the contrary, it had left Lisa with chills and her throat filled with bile.

It can't be true. She couldn't possibly know all this.

But she did. She sat there in front of Lisa and told her exactly how much she knew, and it was too much. Way too much.

Lisa rose to her feet, then walked to the window and looked down at the parking lot where she saw Emma walk to her car. Lisa had always loathed the woman, but now it was more than that. Now she knew she had to get her out of the way.

"She knows too much," she mumbled. "She knows more than is good for her. She needs to be stopped."

There was a light knock on the door, and her assistant peeked in. She smiled nervously. "Lisa?"

Lisa didn't turn to look at her. Her eyes were fixated on Emma Frost below the window. "What is it?"

Louise cleared her throat. "The delegation from Russia has landed. The driver is asking if they should be taken to city hall right away or go to their hotel first?"

Lisa turned to look at the woman. She wanted to meet them, yes. And she ought to be the first one there to greet them. But she was shaken up right now, and it needed to be taken care of. She simply couldn't have that woman running around freely with all that she knew. It could prove to be a catastrophe if she told anyone.

Imagine if she went to the media!

"Take them to the hotel first, please," Lisa said, putting on her nice tone. "I'll meet with them later."

"Okay. I'll let the driver know," Louise said.

Lisa glared down at the parking lot and Emma Frost as she got into her car and took off. Lisa bit her nails frantically while thinking about how to approach this.

"And hold my meetings for the rest of the morning," Lisa said, then grabbed her purse.

Her assistant gave her a strange look. "Hold all your meetings, but how will—?"

"Just do it. Tell them I have a sick child; come up with something and prove yourself useful for once. Have an original thought, will you? You millennials should be able to come up with something more original than avocado toast, for crying out loud!"

Lisa hissed at her as she rushed past her into the lobby and out of city hall, clacking along on her high heels. She spotted Emma's car as it stopped at the end of the parking lot, then turned left on the street leading toward the harbor.

Lisa found her own car keys, then clicked her Volkswagen open and jumped in. The engine came to life, and she took off following Emma's red car close, yet not so close that she'd get suspicious.

FIFTY-FIVE

"Thomas? I don't know if you remember me."

Maya stared at the pale man in the doorway of his house. His eczema was acting up, and he had red patches on his chin and cheek, probably due to the excessive cold and dryness they were experiencing right now.

"Yes," he said with a slight smile. "I remember you. You were at one meeting last winter, right? With that guy, the tall, handsome one."

She nodded, shivering slightly at the memory of the man she had believed was her boyfriend but turned out to be the one who had murdered their best friend and drunk all his blood. Luckily, he was gone now.

"Yes, that was me."

"How can I help you? We're not having a meeting today. We have one scheduled a week from now if you want to join us."

She shook her head. "I'm afraid I can't wait that long. Do you have a minute?"

"Sure," he said. "Come on in. I just made a fresh pot of

coffee; that can help warm us up. It's colder than ever today, even though that doesn't seem possible."

"I'd like that. Thank you."

He showed her inside, and she recognized the place from when she had been at the meeting. The banners and signs were down, and there were no chairs in a circle in the living room, but other than that, it looked the same as it had back then.

"Please sit," he said and pointed at a worn-out couch. She did as he told her, and he brought them each a cup of hot coffee. Maya warmed her hands on the sides of the cup. The bike ride to his house on her lunch break from work had been excruciatingly cold, and her fingertips were almost numb. Yet she felt herself getting warmed up slightly in his house now, and that made her feel calmer.

The fear of having gotten the virus made her almost sick to her stomach, but all day today, she had felt better, and she was beginning to think that maybe she wasn't as sick as she had believed initially. Maybe not everyone got really sick from this. Maybe it was just some people.

Maya blinked to get the images of Jannik and the girl to go away. There was so much she didn't understand. Like how did Ingrid manage somehow to freeze that guy she touched on the head? Maya could still hear the sound of his skin cracking as it froze. It was truly amazing and frightening at the same time.

"What can I do for you?" he asked. "I have a feeling you haven't come here because you've had an encounter, am I right?"

She nodded with a sniffle. "But I have seen things, stuff lately that makes me believe that something strange is truly going on around here."

"I know what you mean," he said and leaned back on the couch. "Take this excruciating cold, for instance. There's something about it that tells me it's related to the abductions. Is that why you're here?"

She nodded. "Partly. See, I need to find someone, and she usually comes here to your group."

"I can't give you information on a group member," he said. "Everything here is confidential."

"I know. I know. But it's just well... it's very important that I find her. My brother has the same... disease as her, and I recently saw her do something that I... I can't explain, and..."

Thomas bit his lip. "You're not making much sense. Now, I'm used to that in here, but maybe you should tell me the entire story. From the beginning. Please."

FIFTY-SIX

I couldn't help myself. I drove past Fishy Pines just to see if I could see my son. But the guard there stopped me at the entrance.

"You know better than that."

"I just want to make sure he's all right, please?"

But, of course, he wouldn't budge, and I had to leave again before I punched the guy, and it all ended in a bad way for me. I got back in the car, where I sat for a few minutes, looking through my pictures of Victor on my phone, missing him terribly.

Then I started the old car again, and it coughed but didn't start. I really should get a newer car, I thought, as I tried again. It wasn't very safe, especially not for the children, and it didn't even have airbags in case we crashed. It wasn't like I couldn't afford a newer car. I just loved this old one so much.

I drove out of the parking lot. As I went back onto the road, I noticed a yellow Volkswagen Beetle parked on the road. As soon as I started driving, it took off as well.

I kept my eyes on it in my mirrors, then shook my head and

told myself I was just being paranoid. I looked at my watch and decided to go home to Daniel, who had to be all alone at the house because Maya had an early shift today. Daniel was good at being alone; I think he enjoyed it, but I didn't like leaving him. I had, after all, promised his mother to keep an eye on him.

"Where are you, Lyn?" I mumbled as I took a turn, then peeked into my rearview mirror and realized the Beetle did the same. Puzzled at this, I took another turn and went for another route home, just to see if it followed me.

It did. A few seconds after I took the turn, it did as well. Was I being followed?

"Who the heck would want to follow me?" I asked myself. "And why?"

I decided to take another detour just to drive whoever was in that Beetle crazy. I went through the neighborhood three times before it finally gave up and I lost it.

Laughing at this, I took off and went toward my house. It had started snowing again as I took the turn onto my street and could spot my house at the end of the road.

My beautiful old house.

I had come to love the place so much. In my heart, I knew I never wanted to leave. This was my home now, even with all the strangeness, the secrets, and the weird people it came with. This was where I belonged.

I smiled to myself, thinking I would never have thought I'd feel at home in a place like this. Had someone told me that years ago, when I still lived in Copenhagen, I would have laughed. I would have told them they were stark raving mad.

Home is not just where I go to bed.

I had never understood that until I got to the island. There was so much more to this home than just the house. It was also my friends on the island. It was Sophia, Jack, Dr. Williamsen, and, of course, Mort...

I never got to finish the thought. Something moved in the corner of my eye, and I turned to look. In the second I did, my world exploded. In a rain of glass and excruciating noise, everything was turned upside down, and I felt nothing but pain so deep it seemed impossible. I didn't even get to scream before it all went dark, and I swam away in a sea of stars.

FIFTY-SEVEN

Ingrid watched it happen. She wished she hadn't. She wished she had stayed in the basement and not gone up into the kitchen to grab some food, but it was too late now. She had just stolen a couple of slices of bread and put jam on them, then grabbed a couple of cold sodas from the fridge to take with her downstairs when she saw the car come driving up the street.

At first, everything about the scene seemed normal. It was the owner of the house she was hiding in who was coming home, and Ingrid knew she had to hurry and hide. But then she spotted the yellow car, the Beetle, as it came from her left side. It all happened so fast, yet Ingrid managed to think so much before it really did.

Watch out!

CRASH!

Ingrid didn't even cover her eyes. She saw it all happen, watched every little detail of it with great terror. Then she dropped the bread and sodas and rushed outside. She stopped at the doorstep, heart throbbing in her throat as the driver of the yellow car opened the door. Blood was running from her forehead, but she seemed to be okay otherwise. She staggered out into the street, then walked up to the other car. It had been pushed into the side of the road by the crash and had run into a streetlamp. The entire front of it was completely smashed.

The woman from the yellow car peeked into the smashed car, and Ingrid considered for a second running to help, but there was something about this woman that made her hesitate.

What is she doing?

Ingrid expected her to try to get the other driver out, to try to help the woman in the other car, the woman who owned the house that Ingrid hid in. She expected her to at least try to call for help. But for some reason, she didn't do any of that. Instead, she peeked inside the other car, then reached a hand in, but soon retracted it again. Then she looked around her as if to see if anyone had seen them. Then she turned around and took off running.

What on earth?

She didn't seem to have noticed Ingrid standing there, and rushed down the street, wiping the blood off her forehead. Ingrid watched her come closer, then bent down behind the hedge so she wouldn't be seen, and as she came really close, hurrying for the trees to cover her, Ingrid recognized her.

The mayor!

She had seen the mayor on her parents' TV and the cover of the local newspaper many times. She had even seen her speak at some event downtown that her parents dragged her to as well. There was no doubt in her mind that it was her.

What was she doing? Was she just going to run away?

Ingrid stared at her, then tried to get up, but as she did, she made a rustle, and the mayor stopped. She turned her head and looked in the direction of where Ingrid was. Ingrid held her breath while hiding behind the barren hedge, hoping it would still cover her.

The mayor stared in her direction for what felt like a very long time but probably wasn't. It felt like the mayor's eyes were looking directly at her, and Ingrid's heart started to pound so violently she feared the mayor could hear it too.

Please, don't see me. Please.

As if she had heard her, the mayor shook her head and moved on. She continued, lightly jogging as she disappeared between the trees. Ingrid finally dared to get up, and she ran back into the house. She had gotten rid of her phone, so the police couldn't track her and come for her, but inside, she found a landline and called for help.

FIFTY-EIGHT

Lisa stopped running. It would only look suspicious if someone saw her, and she couldn't have that. She used her sleeve to wipe the blood from her forehead and felt the bruise. It wasn't too bad. But it had made her realize that what she did could have had serious consequences. She could have killed herself.

The decision had come on the spur of the moment. It wasn't thought through properly. She just knew that she had to shut the woman up before she was able to tell someone what she knew.

It had been a rash decision and a dangerous one. It wouldn't happen again. But now that it was done, she was happy to conclude that it was over. She had peeked into the car and seen her lying there, her face smeared with blood. A big piece of glass had penetrated her chest, and when Lisa reached in to feel for a pulse, there was none.

Emma Frost was dead. Finally.

The feeling of relief was overwhelming, and she couldn't help smiling to herself. Lisa had wanted to get rid of that awful woman for years, and now she finally had. Nothing and no one could stop her now.

She sped up to get away from the neighborhood quicker, yet without running when she heard a sound that made her stop—a rustle behind the hedge surrounding Emma Frost's awful old house. Lisa had always thought that old eyesore should have been demolished many years ago, and maybe now that she was gone, she'd get the chance to tear it down.

Lisa stared between the branches in the hedge but couldn't see anything. She kept looking to make sure, then decided she had to get out of there, fast before someone saw her. She turned around and rushed toward the tall trees, and as soon as she was covered by them, knowing no one could see her now, she pulled out her phone and called a number.

"Hello? Police? This is Mayor Lisa Rasmussen. I want to report my car stolen. It was taken from the parking lot at city hall while I was in a meeting. Yes, earlier this morning. A yellow Volkswagen, yes, I have the license plate number. It's Y-T-five-six-seven-eight-seven."

Lisa gave them the information they needed and hung up with a smile. In the distance, she could hear sirens approaching, and that left her puzzled. Had someone called emergency services already? It had to have been a neighbor. Maybe someone heard the crash and then rushed out. Had they seen Lisa? She sure hoped not.

If they did, it was their word against hers, and guess who the police would believe. There were always people trying to smear her campaign for reelection. This was just another one trying to get her down with their fake stories. Lisa made a tsk sound with her tongue and shook her head.

Then she rushed through the trees until she reached the beach and continued walking that way back to town, looking like she just took a casual stroll—taking a breather between meetings.

Lisa pulled off the scarf from her neck and tied it around her forehead to cover the bruise as she walked up to the main street, greeting people on her way with a pointing finger, saying, "Don't forget, *your* vote matters!"

PART IV

FIFTY-NINE

Maya woke up with a gasp. It felt like her entire body was convulsing as she took a deep breath and her chest heaved up and down. Desperation rushed through her body, and her heart felt like it was going to explode.

Where am I?

Maya forced her eyelids to open, even though they felt so heavy that they barely could. The light was so bright, she had to squint her eyes, but as she did, she soon got used to it, and that was when she realized that she wasn't anywhere she recognized.

What is this place?

She tried to sit up, but as she did, she found out she was strapped to a bed and couldn't move at all. Maya soon panicked and started to yell. "Help! Thomas? Where are you, Thomas?"

He was the last person she remembered seeing. She had been in his house, telling him her story about Ingrid and Daniel and even Victor. Thomas had been nodding, listening carefully, and she had felt like she could tell him all of it, even about Samuel and Lyn, the water creature she knew had escaped from the lab out of town belonging to Omicon. That was when

Thomas had gotten to his feet, then told her he'd get her something to drink, and she had accepted a soda. As she drank her Coke, she had felt dizzy, and then she didn't remember anything else.

Had there been something in that soda? Had Thomas put it in there? Had he brought her here?

"Thomas?"

She lifted her head and spotted him standing not far from her, then called his name again. He didn't react, and as she stopped, she could hear him talking. There was someone with him, standing with his back turned to her, wearing a long white doctor's coat.

"I didn't know what to do with her," she heard Thomas say. "So, I brought her here. She knows too much—like way too much. I couldn't let her go back out there and tell. She's dangerous."

"You did well, Thomas, thank you. That's why we had you set up the group in the first place, so you could keep an eye on our subjects and make sure they didn't get close to the truth."

"And none of them have so far. The story about alien abductions fits well with what they experience and is easy for them to accept. There's the matter of Tony Larsen, though," he said. "He claimed to have woken up in the middle of the experiment, but I think I managed to get him to believe he hadn't seen things right. Besides, I don't think anyone will believe him. He doesn't hold a lot of credibility around the island."

"Good work," the white coat said and handed him a stack of bills. "Thank you."

Maya watched as Thomas walked away, counting his money while she called his name, but he could obviously not hear her. Or he chose not to. The man he had talked to turned around and approached her. As he stepped into the light, Maya could see who he was. Seeing his stern face that she had looked at so many times at the dinner table at Alex's house made her heart drop.

Dr. Finnerup leaned forward and looked down at her, then smiled.

"We'll take good care of you here, sweetie. Don't you worry."

SIXTY

Ingrid was crushed. She didn't know what to do. The house was cold and empty. She still hid in the basement, but no one came home the next day or the day after that, so she finally snuck up into the kitchen to get some food. She felt tears pile up in her eyes as she thought about the woman in the car, the woman she knew from the photos on the refrigerator where she was smiling while holding her children.

She felt like she knew her so well after hiding in the house for days. She felt like she knew them all—knew their routines. She had snuck around in the house when they left and looked at photos in the living room and stolen some of their books and magazines to keep her entertained while hiding out.

But the past two days, none of them had come home—not the mother, which she knew why, of course, because she was dead. But the girl hadn't come home either, and that left Ingrid puzzled. Had she gone somewhere else to sleep so she wouldn't be alone now that her mom was dead? Was she with that boyfriend of hers? Ingrid had seen him come and pick her up and saw them kissing in his car. She had caught herself wishing she was Maya, and that she had her life.

"Who are you?"

Ingrid turned around with a light gasp and looked into the very blue eyes of a young boy who had walked into the kitchen without her hearing him. She couldn't stop staring at him because he kept changing. His skin seemed wobbly, and his hands turned to liquid, then back to solid form again.

"I'm Ingrid," she said with a soft smile. "Who are you?"

"I'm Daniel." The boy looked at Ingrid's blue lips and her frost-covered skin. "You're cold, aren't you?"

She nodded. "Yes, very."

"You're the reason why this house is freezing again, aren't you? You're like Victor."

She nodded again. "Yeah. I'm sorry about that. I've been staying in the basement because I'm hiding out."

Now it was his turn to nod, except his neck and face turned liquid as he did, so the movement became strange and was accompanied by a slushing sound. His face turned solid again.

"I'm hiding too," he said. "I bet it's from the same people."

"I think you're probably right," she said.

His eyes wandered and landed on the bread on the counter. "I'm hungry."

"Yeah, well, me too. How about we toast some of this old bread and eat it with jam and butter?"

"I'd like that."

She grabbed the bread and put a couple of slices in the toaster.

Daniel stared out the window into the street. "No one has come home for days. Do you know where they are?"

Ingrid's eyes hit the floor. She closed them briefly, thinking about the crashed cars in the street and the woman. She had watched as they pulled her out of the car and put her on the ground. She had seen the police officer try to revive her by giving her mouth-to-mouth, then shaking his head.

She was dead.

"I don't," she lied. "Maybe they'll be back soon, huh?"

The bread popped up from the toaster, and she grabbed the slices, then put them on a plate. As she turned to look at Daniel, she saw someone outside the window, looking in, eyes wide and a smug smile on her face. The sight made Ingrid drop the plate to the tile floor, where it shattered. Yet it could barely be heard over the sound of stomping boots.

SIXTY-ONE

"Quick. Run."

Ingrid looked down at Daniel. His terrified eyes stared back up at her like he expected her to save him somehow. The boots sounded like they had surrounded the entire house, and now the front door was kicked in.

"Turn to liquid if they try to grab you, okay? Now, RUN!"

She yelled at the boy to make him understand, and he did. He turned around and took off, running out of the kitchen. Out of the windows, Ingrid saw more men dressed in black, wearing full body armor.

Ingrid knew she wouldn't make it out. She would try to fight her way, using her freeze powers, but there was no way she could outrun them, so she stayed put in the kitchen. She grabbed a Post-it note, then wrote a message for whoever might find it, then stuck it to the fridge.

As she heard the boots come closer, and the door was opened, she readied herself, holding out both her hands, working up a wave of anger big enough. She had been practicing in the basement, freezing things on command and had gotten quite good at it.

The first man in black entered, and Ingrid took a deep breath, then focused. He approached her, holding out a gun, yelling loudly.

"I've got her. In here!"

Ingrid walked closer, holding up her hands like she was surrendering herself, but the guy must have known what she was capable of because he recoiled. Ingrid smiled, then reached down and touched the tip of the weapon, and immediately it froze.

"What the...?" the man yelled and dropped the gun as the frost traveled up its back. The gun fell to the floor, frozen solid, and now the man felt it in his fingers too, where he had been holding the gun. He cursed, then took off his gloves, and they both watched as the frost traveled up his arm, freezing every part of him on the way.

"Stay back! Stay back!" he yelled, his voice cracking with fear. "Help! In here, help!"

Ingrid tilted her head and watched as the arm froze, and it traveled through his body, then felt amazed at her own powers and how strong she had become. This was just from her using the tip of her finger. She knew her power was growing because she felt it in her body, but she had no idea that she was capable of doing something like this.

The man's backup arrived just as he grabbed his chest and fell to his knees, and the frost traveled up his throat and face, then froze him in what looked like a scream, making an ice sculpture of him.

"Whoa," one of the others said, and they all pushed back, pointing their guns at her.

Ingrid smiled, still while maintaining the anger ready under the surface, when the door opened again, and someone peeked inside.

"We got the boy."

He was carrying what looked like a vacuum cleaner. He

lifted the tank, and she could see it was filled with water. Ingrid saw Daniel's eyes inside of it, and her heart dropped. They had sucked him up in that thing. They knew what he was capable of and had come prepared.

"Let him go," Ingrid yelled. "I'll freeze all of you!"

The door opened again, and in trotted the mayor. Two other men followed her. Between them, they were holding a big plastic tube.

"Let me deal with this one," she said, and the men rushed out, dragging their frozen buddy with them. She nodded at the two other men, and they rushed to Ingrid, coming at her fast, then sinking the tube down above her, like trapping a spider in a glass.

Terrified, Ingrid touched the sides of the tube, trying to freeze it, then break it, but it didn't work. The mayor pressed on her phone, and a bottom layer shot out, trapping Ingrid's legs above the knees, so she could still move her feet just enough to walk.

The mayor stepped forward, grinning.

"Amazing what you can do with an app these days, huh? Now, you can fight it all you want, but you won't be able to get out. It's plastic. Low-density polyethylene. Also known as thermoplastic. Resistant to extreme temperatures. Remains impact resistant even when frozen. It can sustain temperatures minus eighty-four degrees Celsius and should keep us all safe."

Ingrid growled and snorted while ice crystals spurted out of her nostrils. "What do you want from me?"

"You thought I didn't see you out there, didn't you? On the day of the crash when you were hiding in the bushes, but I did see you. I just didn't want you to know. I wanted to come back for you, prepared, and have been watching the house since I saw you and realized it was harboring more fugitives. See, you're both very valuable to me, especially you, my dear."

"I don't care," Ingrid hissed. "I don't want to have anything to do with you."

"Oh, well, now, there's no reason to be nasty. I think you and I could be good friends if you gave it a shot. I know I am very interested in you, my dear. The thing is, you're supposed to be dead by now. All our other test subjects died within the first week or two after we injected the serum into them, but you're still here, somehow, and you're not even sick. In fact, you have been busy, haven't you? Freezing the people I sent for you. It's truly marvelous. You are worth a lot of money, my dear, billions, and now it's time for you to come home.

"You work for me now, you hear me? You do as I tell you or the boy will feel the pain. You have already caused so much grief around here. Think of your parents and the woman, this wonderful woman who lived here, who harbored you and the boy. She's gone now. All because of you. You don't want to cause any more pain, do you?"

She paused, looking into Ingrid's eyes. Ingrid's shoulders slumped, and she exhaled deeply while thinking of her poor parents and all they had been through. The mayor was right. Enough was enough. Ingrid had to think of others more than just herself.

"I didn't think so," the mayor said, then signaled her men. Ingrid didn't even scream as they lifted her in the tube and carried her out of the house. She didn't have the energy.

Ingrid knew when she was beaten.

SIXTY-TWO

"I think she's waking up."

The words echoed in my mind, and I couldn't determine what direction they came from. They sounded far away, like they belonged in a different world—the one outside of my mind, the one on the other side of my closed eyelids.

Morten!

My eyelids were heavy and almost impossible to open, but I forced them anyway. Even though the long arms of sleep tried to lure me back, I knew I had to look at him.

"Emma?"

"M-Morten?"

"You're here; you're really there." He was crying, almost sobbing, and at first, I didn't understand why. Not until I looked around me and realized I was in a hospital bed, monitors beeping next to me, hooked up to all kinds of tubes.

"I thought we had lost you," he said, tears still running down his cheeks. "Don't ever do that to me again."

"W-where am I? What happened?"

Dr. Williamsen stepped forward so I could see him standing by the end of my bed. "You're at my clinic. We couldn't get you to the mainland hospital because of the ice, but we were going to airlift you later today. Guess we won't need to, now that you've woken up. Good to see your beautiful eyes again, Emma, I must say. You had me worried there."

Mrs. Williamsen came up behind him and grabbed his arm, then smiled at me. "We were all very worried there."

Morten grabbed my hand in his and caressed it gently while wiping his tears away with the other hand. "You were in a car accident. Someone rammed straight into you, then took off on foot. We never found out who it was. Do you recall anything about what happened?"

I tried to remember but came up blank. I wrinkled my forehead with concern.

"I... I don't think I do."

"It might come back to you later," Dr. Williamsen said. "Just give it some time. You need lots of rest. You experienced a severe concussion and had a piece of glass penetrate the skin on your chest. Luckily, it didn't go very deep, and it didn't penetrate anything important in there."

"Guess it helped to be fat for once, huh?" I said with a scoff, then felt the bandage on my chest. It hurt to move my arm, so I put it down. "How long have I been out?"

"It's been two days," Morten said. "The longest two days of my life."

"Morten has been here by your side and barely left since you were brought in, even at night, the dear heart," Mrs. Williamsen said with a mischievous smile. I knew she wanted Morten and me to get back together. Most people on the island felt that way, but it wasn't that simple.

"And Maya? What about Maya?" I asked. "Where is she?"

Morten looked down at his shoes, then back up at me. "She's been missing for two days too. She was the first one I called, and she never picked up. I kept trying and got really worried. I had my colleagues go to your house, but she wasn't there. No one opened the door when they knocked. I had them go look for her at the gas station, but she had missed her shift. They said she left on her lunch break two days ago but never came back. I was very worried, so I had someone trace her phone, and it was found in a rubbish bin by the old fishing museum.

"Are you telling me my daughter is missing?" I tried to sit up but couldn't and had to lie back down. My head was pounding like crazy, and it felt like it was going to explode.

"You really do need to take it easy," Dr. Williamsen said.

Morten exhaled and rubbed his stubble. He hadn't shaved in days. "I am afraid so."

I struggled to keep calm. I couldn't just lie here while my daughter might be in trouble. I tried to sit up again but only made it up on my elbow.

"Did you ask Alex? Her boyfriend?"

Morten nodded. "He hasn't seen her either. I am sorry. I know it's a lot right now."

"Do you think it's connected?" I asked. "Me being in an accident and her disappearing?"

He shrugged. "It could be a coincidence, but it is kind of strange. I get the feeling someone is out to get you. We checked the scene of the crash. There were no skid marks on the asphalt. The street had been cleared of snow recently by one of the plows from city hall, so that wasn't the problem either. This person didn't even try not to ram into you. It was done intentionally."

"But they left the car? Can't you find out who owns it and then figure out who it was?" I asked.

"I'm afraid the car had been reported stolen," he said. "So that doesn't really help."

I sank back into my pillow, wishing someone would just cut my head off so it wouldn't hurt so terribly. I felt like crying as I didn't like being so helpless. It overwhelmed me, and, at the same time, my body was aching so deeply, I just wanted to go back to sleep. But I didn't cry. Instead, I felt the anger as it rose inside me. All the worried eyes in the room were on me now, and I knew they'd never let me go out and look for my daughter. Not in my condition.

"I think I need to rest now," I said, closing my eyes briefly, then opening them again like I was struggling to stay awake. "I'm really tired, and my head hurts."

"I'll give you something for that pain," Dr. Williamsen said. "I'll give you something to help you sleep too. It's been a lot for now."

"We'll leave you to rest. All of us," Mrs. Williamsen said and pulled Morten by the hand, so he'd understand that meant him too. He smiled nervously, then looked at me while the doctor gave me my pills and a drink of water.

"Thank you for all your help," I said to Morten. He was about to leave when I stopped him. "Say, just one thing before you go. Who is the owner of the car, the one that was stolen and then rammed into me?"

Morten looked at me again. "Oh, it was the mayor's."

I stared at him, clenching my fists hard, just now remembering my visit to her office shortly before the accident.

"You don't say?"

He nodded. "Yeah, apparently, it was stolen from the parking lot at city hall while she was in a meeting."

"What a coincidence that it would be her car, huh?" I asked.

He nodded, then put on his hat. "Yeah, well... I guess so. Now, sleep well, Emma. I'll check in on you later."

"You do that. And thank you, Morten."

He smiled, then walked out, saying, "Anything for you, Emma. You know that."

SIXTY-THREE

"The Chinese are getting restless."

Lisa had barely entered city hall before Camilla jumped up from the couch and sprang toward her. Lisa glared at her assistant, then grabbed Camilla by the shoulder.

"Let's take it in my office, shall we? Louise, hold my calls."

"You promised them a demonstration days ago," Camilla continued as they walked in and closed the door behind them. "They're anxious and are threatening to leave."

Lisa put her briefcase down. "Well, if they do leave now, they'll be missing out on something great, and we can't have that now, can we? You tell them that."

Louise had left a stack of messages on her desk, and she went through them quickly to make sure there wasn't something important. None of it seemed to be worthy of her time. She had better and more important things to take care of than all that small-town stuff that people kept bothering her with—like wanting a new parking garage downtown or wanting to buy more snowplows to cope with the excessive amount of snow they had gotten so far this year.

Didn't they know that if all went well with Lisa's plans, they could buy a hundred new snowplows and have as many parking garages as they wanted?

Of course, they didn't. No one on the island thought big enough. That's why they needed her. They would soon come to understand that.

"That's what I've been telling them, but it's not enough anymore," Camilla groaned. "You promised them proof, and all you've given them is empty talk. I'm not sure I can get them to stay any longer. The Chinese are threatening to leave tomorrow. So are the Russian and North Korean delegations. They feel like you've been stalling them for way too long and no longer believe you actually have a product to sell."

Lisa raised her head and smiled. "Well, let them because the demonstration will be tonight. And you tell them that it'll be spectacular. We just had something special come in, something that will blow their minds."

Camilla's eyes grew wide. "So, tonight?"

"Yes, Camilla, tonight. That's what I just said."

"So, just to be completely certain that I got it right, there'll be a demonstration tonight where they'll see the product in action."

Lisa shook her head with a scoff. "Yes, Camilla. Tonight. Do you have issues with your hearing? You might want to have that looked into. Have them arrive at seven o'clock, and we'll have the champagne ready. The highest bidder gets to go home with the product in hand. It'll be worth their long wait. Believe me; they'll think so too."

Camilla, relieved, exhaled and folded her hands together. "Thank you. Finally, I can give them some good news. I'll go to the hotel and tell them this right away."

Camilla left, and Lisa sat down in her chair, looking at her screen while biting the inside of her cheek. She couldn't help feeling a little nervous about tonight. It was only natural to have butterflies in her stomach. This was, after all, what she had worked on for years.

Tonight was going to be the most important in her entire life. There was no room for failure. Nothing could go wrong. Nothing.

SIXTY-FOUR

Barely had the door closed behind Morten and the Williamsens before I sat up in bed. I spat out the sleeping pills that I had hidden in my cheek while pretending to swallow them.

I unhooked myself from the drip, then got out of bed and threw the sleeping pills in the rubbish bin next to me while the painkiller kicked in. I was wearing a hospital gown but found my bloody clothes on a chair and put them on. It hurt like crazy when I tried to move my arm, but somehow, I managed to get dressed.

I walked to the window, opened it, and slid out into the freezing snow in Dr. Williamsen's garden. I stumbled across the garden, then climbed over the hedge to make sure they couldn't see me from inside the house, then ran into the street, and soon I was staggering along in the thick snow on the sidewalk.

Going home.

I reached my house about twenty minutes later, and my fingertips and legs were freezing as I stumbled into my hallway. Kenneth and Brutus were the first to greet me. Kenneth jumped up and down my leg, while Brutus just sat there and gave me a look that made me feel like the worst mom in the world.

Kenneth had peed on the carpet, I could tell, several times, and had pooped in my shoes. If I knew Brutus right, he had probably used the toilet and even flushed.

"I am sorry, guys. I'll let you out."

I went to the back door, then let them out in the garden. I walked back into the living room, then realized the house felt surprisingly hot, and I turned the radiators down. It was almost like a sauna.

"Daniel?" I yelled, then walked up the stairs, even though my body was aching terribly. I went to his room but didn't find him there. Neither was he in Victor's room where he would sometimes hang out.

"Maya?" I tried, then walked to her room. Not surprisingly, it was empty as well. Morten had told me she was gone. But I had expected to find Daniel. It didn't make me feel good that he was missing too.

What was going on here?

I went to my bedroom, took a shower, and got dressed in some clean clothes. It took forever because of the pain in my chest and arm, not to mention my head, but the painkiller that the doctor had given me was working surprisingly well, and soon I was dressed and had washed all the blood off my face. I had some horrible bruises, but hopefully, they'd go away over time. The scar on my chest would remain, though. It would forever remind me of what happened, even though I didn't remember the details.

It was following me, wasn't it? The yellow Beetle.

I looked at my face in the mirror while it was beginning to come back to me.

Yes, it was. It was following me from city hall, where I left after meeting with Lisa Rasmussen. Where I had just told her everything I knew. How had I been so stupid?

I heard a noise coming from downstairs and rushed toward the stairs. "Maya?"

A face appeared at the bottom of the stairs, but it wasn't Maya. It was Sophia.

"Emma? You're back? Morten told me what happened. I am so sad I wasn't home to see it. Are you okay?"

I held on to the rail as I walked down the steps, leaning on it because of the pain.

"You don't look too well, Emma. Are you sure you shouldn't be in bed?" Sophia asked, as I came down and leaned on her for support.

"I'm fine. I just... I need to know where my daughter is. And Daniel. He's missing too."

"Christoffer said something about seeing a bunch of black vans parked in your driveway and some military types entering your house yesterday afternoon. He was home alone, so, unfortunately, I didn't see anything. He thought it might be the police, but it didn't say police on the vans."

I stared at my friend while trying to get the pieces to fit together. Who would just come here and take Daniel? Had the same people taken Maya as well?

"Emma? You're very pale," Sophia said. "Don't you want to go sit down? Here, let me help you into the kitchen."

"I could drink some water," I said, as she helped me get to a chair in the kitchen. Sophia grabbed a glass and filled it with water. The kitchen was a mess. The table was pushed to the other end by the sinks, and the floor was covered in dirty footprints that looked like they came from boots.

"Someone tried to clean up after them, trying to hide that they were here," I said. "Everything is in the wrong place."

Sophia handed me the glass of water, and I drank from it when I saw something attached to the fridge, something that wasn't usually there. I rose to my feet and approached it, squinting my eyes to see what was on the yellow Post-it note.

"What is it?" Sophia asked.

"This note," I said and pointed at it. "It's not usually here."

"What does it say?"

I stared at it. "Tony Larsen. Who is Tony Larsen?"

Sophia shrugged.

"It's not Maya's handwriting, at least it doesn't look like it. Someone must have thought it important enough to put it up there, putting it in a place where no one would think it was a message and take it down when cleaning up after themselves. Whoever did this wanted me to find it."

I grabbed the note and pulled it down, then glared at the name. "Tony Larsen. Could he have taken Maya? And Daniel maybe?"

"Why would he tell you then?" Sophia asked.

"Nah, you have a point," I said pensively. "Let's pay him a visit and find out."

SIXTY-FIVE

The weather had turned nastier, even though it seemed like it couldn't get worse than it already was. A winter-like storm was sweeping over the island, bringing more snow and freezing temperatures. On the car radio, while Sophia was driving toward Tony Larsen's house, the announcers were warning people against going out in what could turn out to be dangerous conditions and especially driving on the icy roads.

Sophia slid up into Tony's driveway, almost going sideways before she managed to stop. I opened the door and shuddered as the icy winds hit my face. We hurried up to the front door, barely avoiding slipping on the way. It felt like even my eyebrows were frozen when I rang the doorbell.

Sophia shivered and blew on her hands, even though she was wearing gloves. Her breath remained in the air like a cloud in front of her face.

"Hurry up, please," she mumbled. "It's cold."

I rang the doorbell again.

"What do we do when he opens the door?" Sophia asked. "I mean, we suspect he has taken the kids, right? Or that he at least knows what happened to them."

I shrugged, then bit my lip. It felt numb from the cold. I had to admit I hadn't really thought about what to do. I just knew I had to find this guy and hoped it would lead me to the children's whereabouts—that somehow this guy knew who had taken them or where they were.

"Hello? Is anyone home?" I said, then knocked on the door hard and slightly desperate. "Please, open up!"

Still, nothing.

I growled, annoyed, then walked to the window and pressed my nose against the glass, placing my hands to cover my eyes so I could peek inside. I glanced around the living room when my eyes fell on something in the hallway, sticking out in the doorway.

Feet.

I gasped and pulled back, then looked at Sophia.

"What? What did you see?"

"We need to get in there."

I grabbed the door handle and turned it. It was freezing cold and hurt my hand through the glove, but as I pushed it down, I realized the door was unlocked.

Something was blocking the door from the other side though, and Sophia had to help me push it open. We put all our weight into it and managed to get it open just enough for me to squeeze in. On the floor, behind the door, I found a man. Sophia squeezed herself in behind me, and now we stood there, staring at the poor guy on the floor of his hallway.

"His hand is reaching for the door," Sophia said.

"Like he was trying to get out," I said and swallowed.

"What do you think happened?" she asked.

I knelt next to him, then looked at the marks on his throat and face. "He froze to death," I said. "Look at that frostbite. It's all over his fingers too. Just like Lars Madsen. I'd say he froze to death from the inside out."

"Black frost," Sophia said with a light gasp.

"Exactly," I said and nodded, then rose to my feet. "We were too late."

A noise coming from the living room made me turn to look.

"What was that?" Sophia asked.

"I don't know," I said, "but there it was again. It sounds like scraping of some sort. Come on."

I walked toward the doorway leading to the living room when Sophia whimpered lightly. "Are you sure? It sounds creepy."

I didn't listen to her; I just stepped inside the living room where I saw the most adorable bulldog lying on the floor. It was using its paws to scrape on the wooden floor.

"It's a dog," Sophia said, relieved.

"It's not well," I said and approached it. "It's been left in here for quite some time. We need to help it."

I walked to the dog, then knelt. It was scraping weakly on the floor like it was signaling for me to help it.

"Quick, get some water," I said.

Sophia went to the kitchen and put water in a bowl that she brought for the dog, while I looked at the tag on his collar.

"Buddy, huh? We'll get you up and running again, my friend; don't you worry."

Sophia brought the water, and it started to drink, at first weakly, then faster and more vigorously. Soon, it rose to its feet; even though it looked a little like Bambi on the ice, it soon found out how to regain balance.

"There you go, little friend."

I patted it on the top of its head when my eyes fell on something behind it. Up against the back wall of the room leaned a row of freshly made paintings. I approached them and glared down at them.

"What do we have here?" Sophia asked, coming up behind me.

"It... I might be wrong, but it looks like he has been painting... what he... look at this," I said and took one for her to see.

"Look, there are a lot of sketches on the floor here too," I said and showed her a stack of pencil drawings. "They all show the same thing. This guy has been—"

"Experimented on," Sophia said, her eyes growing wide.

I nodded. "It sure looks like it. He's been a human guinea pig, and my guess is no one believed him."

"He was a member of the local UFO group," Sophia said and showed me a pamphlet she found on an end table.

"Except these weren't aliens, and he recently realized that," I said. "Look at the last sketch he made—a very human face staring down at him, holding that syringe."

"You're right," Sophia said.

I stared at the sketch again, then noticed something in the background. "And look at that logo on the wall back there. The big round one."

"Is it Omicon?" Sophia asked.

"Why aren't I surprised? Of course, it is."

Sophia reached out her hands. Her voice grew high as she spoke.

"Oh, my Lord. So, you're telling me that Omicon has been abducting people on this island and using them as human experiments."

I nodded. "My guess is they're the reason people have been freezing to death: Lars, Jannik, the young girl, Ingrid... Victor. And somehow, most died like Tony here. Except for Ingrid and Victor. That's why they're so valuable. That's why they took him from me. Imagine what a weapon they could be if they fell into the wrong hands." I stared at the sketches when another piece fell into place.

"The delegations," I said. "From China, North Korea, and Russia. They're here to buy a weapon. It's been her all along."

"Who?"

"Lisa Rasmussen, the mayor. It all fits into her insane mind. That's why she tried to kill me. I went to her office, and shortly after, I was followed. I remember it now; her car was behind me, the yellow Beetle that she claimed had been stolen. It hit me right after I had almost revealed what she was up to. And Dr. Finnerup is part of it too. He was there right before I went into her office. Lisa and Dr. Finnerup are working together on this, developing a weapon, unlike any other. A child weapon who can walk behind enemy lines, then use their powers to destroy."

"Wow. Really?"

I stared at Sophia. "I know I sound crazy, but I think that is what is going on. The kids from Fishy Pines have been used as experiments, along with random islanders they have abducted and sedated so they'd think it was aliens."

"But what are they putting in them?" Sophia asked. "To make them freeze?"

"My guess is they're using DNA from the water creatures. Remember how Lyn and Samuel told us that they had come here through the sewers because their old world was at war. They came up through the pipes of Fishy Pines, the old, now-condemned part of the building. The plumber who found them was killed that night, remember? Because he had seen too much, and the nurse on duty ended her days in a long-term care facility because she was babbling about the strange creatures from the sewers. My guess is they were locked up there.

"Like Lyn and Daniel, they were taken to the lab and experimented on. They must have extracted DNA from them and tried to apply it to humans. Like Skye, who can lift things just with her mind. That's pretty powerful in a fight. And Lyn, who can turn to liquid and enter any house at any time. The perfect spy. They must have a creature up there who freezes things by touch. If they somehow made a formula or a serum that can give humans those same powers, then it becomes a weapon."

"So, is that why they were testing it on the people they abducted and the kids at Fishy Pines?" Sophia asked.

I nodded. "Yes, because they would never be allowed to test something like that on humans. So, they did it without anyone knowing about it until it suddenly worked."

Sophia clasped her mouth. "Victor?"

I nodded. "Yes. He was sick to begin with but got better. My guess is that's why they took him. They didn't care about his well-being or mental stability. It wasn't what was best for him. He's their best product."

"And their clients just came to town, bringing lots of money," Sophia said.

"Exactly."

SIXTY-SIX

I took Buddy with me in the car, and Sophia stayed behind to give her statement to the police about us finding Tony Larsen. We had cooked up a story that kept me out of it, so I could move on and figure out how to approach my new knowledge.

I drove up in my driveway, then grabbed Buddy in my arms, and carried the dog inside. Kenneth was jumping on me from the second I walked in, and I had to nudge him away because he was crawling up my leg to get to see the new dog I had brought home.

I slammed the door shut behind me, then carried Buddy into the living room, where I put him on the couch. He was still weak, but definitely better. It was late in the day, and the vet was closed by now, so I'd have to take him in the morning.

Kenneth jumped up on the couch and sniffed Buddy's behind eagerly, while Brutus kept his distance. I turned to look at him and could tell he wanted to come closer but didn't dare.

"Come on, Brutus," I said. "Come say hello."

He gave me a shy look, then finally walked up. I moved out of his way, so he could sniff the new dog.

"This is our new friend," I said. "His name is Buddy. You be good to him, you hear me?"

Brutus looked up at me with his light blue eyes, then down at the dog. He started sniffing Buddy eagerly and soon seemed to get very agitated. Now, had this been Kenneth, I wouldn't have reacted, but this was Brutus. He was always calm, barely moved a muscle, or made a sound. Yet today, he was suddenly wagging his tail eagerly and jumping around playfully, almost acting foolish, barking and turning around, grabbing a pillow and biting it, then returning, staring at the dog on the couch, which seemed to enjoy the attention.

"Brutus?" I asked. "What's gotten into you?"

Brutus sniffed Buddy in the private area, and that's when I realized. "Oooh. I guess Buddy is a girl, huh?"

Brutus's eyes had grown wide, and he barked happily. His tongue hung out to the side of his mouth, and it looked like he was almost smiling. That made me laugh.

"I think you're in love, Brutus. Good for you."

I left them to get acquainted, then put out a bowl of food for Buddy before I got myself ready.

It was dark out now and time for me to make my move.

SIXTY-SEVEN

Lisa had all the delegations gathered in a small bunker with glass windows, so they could see everything that took place in the field behind the old Omicon building.

Lisa smiled widely at her guests, then nodded eagerly. "Are you ready to have your minds blown?"

She accompanied her words with hand motions to simulate bombs going off next to her temples and making an exploding noise with her lips.

All eyes looked at her with great confusion. Except for the leader of the Russian delegation, who nodded happily and smiled at her like he expected her to go to bed with him once this was done. He had been looking at her like that ever since she greeted them at her office.

"I think they just want to get to it," Camilla whispered in her ear. "They've waited a long time for this."

"Well, I know that," Lisa snorted. "I just wanted to make an introduction. Besides, the Russians seem to like it."

She smiled and nodded at the guy whose eyes grew even wider in anticipation.

"I don't think he knows any other facial expressions, to be honest," Camilla said.

"Don't be such a party pooper," Lisa said. She grabbed her binoculars and looked toward the area in the middle of the field, where she had instructed them to place her weapon.

The girl was in place, and they had removed the plastic tube that they had kept her in since they took her from Emma Frost's house—the one protecting them from her powers.

Lisa pressed the button on the speaker system, so she could talk directly to the girl.

"Now, you show me all you've got, okay? Remember the talk we had earlier. You have caused enough pain to people who care for you. If you don't do as I told you, the boy will get it. And later, we'll get your parents too. It's all up to you, my dear."

She lifted her finger from the button, then smiled at her guests, nodding. "I think it's ready."

Camilla handed each of them their own binoculars, and Lisa pointed out the window. Then they turned on the lights outside. Nine huge lamps, taken from the local soccer stadium, glowed down at the girl.

The guests lifted their binoculars and looked at her through them. She was standing in the middle of the field, looking frightened. Lisa smiled, then pressed the button again, and said, trying to sound like Michael Keaton from *Beetlejuice,* "It's showtime!"

Lisa laughed at herself, but no one else chimed in. They all remained cool as they stared at the young girl in the middle of a frozen field, while twenty soldiers, fully armored, approached her from all sides.

SIXTY-EIGHT

They came at her from everywhere. No matter where Ingrid looked, she could see them and their weapons that were pointed at her. The sound of the soldiers running toward her was deafening and filled her with great fear.

What is this? What is happening?

With her heart in her throat, she turned around and saw more soldiers coming from behind her, then gasped fearfully.

What do I do? Are they coming to kill me?

That's when a shot was fired. Ingrid screamed as it echoed in the night. The sound came from behind, and she turned just as the bullet left the barrel of the gun.

Without thinking about it, Ingrid lifted her right hand in the air, then sent a wall of ice toward the bullet, stopping it. It was enclosed by the ice and fell to the ground instead of continuing its way toward her.

Seeing this, Ingrid barely breathed. She stepped back, staring at the bullet on the ground that had been so close to her, so incredibly close to killing her. She had no idea where her reaction came from. She hadn't been able to think. It felt like an instinct. Like it was a natural thing for her to do, simply to freeze it.

Ingrid lifted her glare and stared at the soldiers, some of whom had stopped and were staring at the bullet on the ground.

And that was when all hell broke loose.

Suddenly, shots were fired from all sides, and she had to move fast. Turning on her heel, she threw ice toward them, freezing the bullets midair. And soon, she was freezing the soldiers too.

More shots were fired from soldiers coming up behind them, but they too were soon stopped by the ice and fell to the ground, frozen. Then more soldiers came, about twenty or so more, running toward her, boots trampling, and she shot her ice toward them, causing them to fall, frozen in one single movement.

Like it was nothing—like taking a man's life meant nothing.

Panting, she looked around her, glaring to all sides, expecting more to jump at her at any second. She felt mortified that they would send in more. She didn't want to have to hurt more people. When she realized that it was over, and as no more came, she sank to her knees, crying.

"I'm sorry," she said to one of them lying in front of her, his eyes frozen in fear. "I am so, so sorry. They made me do it. They made me!"

SIXTY-NINE

"Yes!"

Lisa clapped her hands together in triumph. The men from the three delegations looked at her, then suddenly started clapping too. Lisa took the applause and bowed, feeling the rush of victory go through her body.

Finally, she had succeeded. Finally.

"Now you've seen what this subject is able to do. Remember, there could have been hundreds of soldiers; she would have killed them all. A thousand more, and she'd have done the same. That's how powerful this girl is, and that's why we keep her in a tube that she can't escape from, or she'd risk killing a lot more people. But imagine sending someone like her into an American base in Afghanistan or Iraq and the havoc she could create. She'd kill everyone in the entire base instantaneously. Heck, send her into an entire town, and she'd destroy them all. Imagine having a weapon like that; you could take over a country within minutes."

This made the Chinese delegates nod with satisfaction. She still wasn't sure she had the North Koreans onboard yet, but she knew her second demonstration would make sure to do just that.

They're going to be eating out of my hand in just a few minutes. And that's when the bidding begins.

"We provide you with the formula, the serum, and you can make as many soldiers like her as you wish. That's what we're selling here today," Lisa continued, almost tasting the billions she would get out of this deal. And this was just the beginning. As soon as more experiments succeeded with all different kinds of powers, she would be providing weapons to the entire world. She'd be the richest woman on earth and Fanoe island the wealthiest place in the world. Maybe they could even separate themselves from the rest of Denmark and become an independent country with Lisa as the leader. Yes, she'd like that. She could be president. Lisa liked the sound of that. President Lisa Rasmussen.

Lisa smiled secretively, then pressed the button again.

"Bring in the next subject. Bring me my moneymaker!"

SEVENTY

I had dressed in all black, which I soon realized was a mistake as I was moving in snow, and I should probably have been in all white in order not to be seen.

I climbed the fence and slid down on the other side, being surprisingly agile for someone like me, and only slightly in pain from my arm and head. Okay, maybe it was a little more than that, but the painkiller did a good job keeping it at bay just enough.

There was a camera on the top of the wall that I kicked down on my way. Then I disappeared into Omicon's huge property, hiding between the trees as the guards came out to see what had happened to the camera. By then, I was long gone, running toward the big lab.

I found a back door that was left ajar and was about to walk inside when I heard loud noises coming from the other end of the property.

Gunshots?

It sounded like a drill was taking place. Boots were trampling, and shots were being fired. It sounded like soldiers rehearsing, but somehow, I knew that wasn't what it was.

It was something far more heartbreaking.

I let go of the door, then ran toward the empty fields behind the lab. It was a long stretch of land, and it took a while for me to get all the way down there, especially with the bad shape I was in. But as more shots were fired, I ran faster, worrying it was my poor Victor who was in trouble.

I came to an old bunker sticking out of the ground, and that's when I saw the lights. Nine super bright stadium lamps were placed in the middle of a field, glowing down on the ground. In the middle of it all, in the snow, sat a young girl on her knees, crying. She was surrounded by dead bodies, dead soldiers, who lay like dead insects on the ground.

The girl was placed in a tube of a sort, then carried away, still weeping, not making any resistance, even though I got the feeling she could. I mean, if she had killed all those soldiers, she could easily kill those who brought the tube, right? But for some reason, she didn't.

Next, I watched as the dead soldiers were dragged away, and the area was cleared.

My question was, for what? What was going to happen next?

I didn't have to wait long for an answer. A clear box was rolled onto the field and opened. Inside sat a young boy, and I watched as he was taken out and left in the middle of the field, underneath the lamps.

My heart nearly stopped.

Victor!

I stared at my son. He just sat there, not even looking up, not even getting up on his feet. It tore me apart.

What are they doing to him?

A loudspeaker somewhere was turned on, and a voice I knew a little too well spoke. "Now, Victor. We know what you can do. I need you to show us, and if you don't, then you know what will happen. We discussed this, remember?"

As the words fell, I heard something and looked in the direction of the noise. Down by the field, not far from where Victor was, I saw several soldiers holding someone between them, a girl. The girl was strapped to what looked like an old-fashioned torture instrument, making it impossible for her to move her hands.

Skye! They're threatening to hurt Skye if he doesn't do what they tell him. My poor boy!

Seeing her, Victor rose to his feet.

Then, I heard a whooshing sound coming from above just as a plane flew toward him. It looked like one of those robotic military planes, a UAV. It lingered above him and got itself in position to shoot. I was prepared to scream when he lifted both his hands and closed his eyes. With the movement he did with his hands, he caused an explosion so big I was thrown into the snow by the soundwaves and the ice that was cast around it. It was like a huge bomb blast, yet with ice.

The drone plane that had been high in the air above him was blown to pieces, and frozen metal plates rained down on the ground surrounding the field.

The plane was gone. Not only that, but it was also vaporized, completely obliterated.

SEVENTY-ONE

"Ha!"

Lisa turned to her guests, smiling widely. "Did you see that? The UAV is gone, annihilated. Imagine this happening in your country. Someone sends in a plane. You shoot it down using someone like Victor here with his powers. No one will ever suspect a thing. No weapons have been fired; it's nothing but a young child. The potential is endless, the sky's the limit. Your limit, if you make us your deliverer of the serum. You can create an arsenal like him. They can blow up tanks, shoot down planes, or blast away buildings. Whatever you like. It'll be all yours."

Now, they were all clapping—even the North Koreans. Lisa smiled and nodded, then shook their hands, one after the other, as they thanked her for the demonstration.

"We will bring bid, first thing in morning," the Chinese leader said in English with a strong accent.

The Russian leader said something in Russian and shook Lisa's hand eagerly before they left.

"The Russians say they'll bring a bid tonight," Dr. Finnerup translated as he approached Lisa, holding out a glass of champagne for her. "And the North Koreans will bid on the boy. They want to buy him too and take him back with them as a prototype. I think it's safe to say your demonstration went well."

Lisa took the champagne and sipped it, satisfied. "Really? Well, if they want the boy, then they'll have to pay a lot more. He's the only one like him so far. He's way stronger than the girl."

"He sure is one of a kind," Dr. Finnerup said. "HP did well recommending him for the trials. I knew that if we found one with his level of mental capacity and intelligence, we just might make this work."

"And you did," Lisa said. "First, you gave him the telekinesis from the girl and then the freeze powers from the frost creature, and boom, you had an exploding cocktail. Well done."

They clinked their glasses, and Lisa sipped more of the champagne. She knew she had promised to share the money with Finnerup once it was on the table, but she wasn't sure she needed him anymore. All his work was documented in their system, and someone else, someone easier to control, could take over from now on with no problems.

"To you, Lisa," he said. "For always thinking big. For daring to." He lifted his glass, and Lisa smiled venomously. As he drank, she spotted an ice pick that someone had left out when putting ice in the bucket for the champagne. She picked it up, then pierced it through his chest, straight through his heart. It sounded an awful lot like puncturing a balloon, she thought, as the man's body fell to the ground with a thud.

SEVENTY-TWO

"Oh, dear Lord," I exclaimed as I finally got back on my feet. My ears were still ringing from the blast. If I didn't have a headache before, I sure had one now. It was pounding worse than when I had been in Dr. Williamsen's clinic. I felt like the air had been blown out of me, and I had trouble standing. It took a while for me to regain my composure and remember where I was.

Once I did, I realized that Victor was gone. The lights had been turned off in the field, and it all seemed like it hadn't happened... like it had all been a dream. An awful, terrible nightmare.

I touched my hurting head and rubbed my temples, closing my eyes briefly to gather myself. When I opened them again, I saw a row of black cars that were driving up to the back side of the bunker. Seconds later, I watched as the delegations rushed to their cars and drove away.

But what about my boy? He had to be here somewhere still, right?

I'm in over my head here. These people have weapons. There is a lot of money at stake here, possibly billions. They're not afraid to kill me if they have to.

"What do I do? I can't leave without my son," I mumbled. "I refuse to. But where do I even find him? This place is monstrous."

Maybe I should get some help.

Thinking I had to go to Morten and tell him what I had seen, make him believe me somehow, maybe force him to come to see for himself, I was about to turn around and walk back when I felt the barrel of a gun pressed against the back of my head and heard it being cocked.

"Hands where I can see them."

I lifted my arms in the air, trembling. Hands from a second guard were on my body, searching me for weapons. The kitchen knife I had brought for protection—for lack of anything better— was pulled out of my trousers.

"You're trespassing; do you know that?" the voice behind me said.

"Really?" I said. "I was just out for a stroll. I must have taken a wrong turn somewhere."

"Is that supposed to be funny?" the other voice said.

"Not really," I said.

"You're coming with us," the one holding the gun behind me said. "Move."

SEVENTY-THREE

"You? I should have known I wouldn't get rid of you that easily."

Lisa Rasmussen snorted when she saw me. The guards had brought me inside the bunker where she was waiting, champagne in her hand. On the floor lay the body of Dr. Finnerup, smeared in blood, an ice pick still jabbed into his chest. I gulped when I saw his wide staring eyes and open mouth, looking like he had a scream stuck inside it.

"Lisa, did you really think no one would figure out what you were doing here?" I asked. "You're not going to get away with it."

She scoffed and sipped her champagne. "I don't care what people think of me."

"That's not what I meant," I said. "You killed a lot of people just as a demonstration. All these people you have experimented on, a lot of them died. Even children. You experimented on my son. You killed Dr. Finnerup. For what? To become rich?"

She turned around and looked at me, madness glowing in her eyes. "Not just plain and ordinary rich, Emma. We're talking filthy wealthy when all the countries in the world will come to me to get their own serum, their own soldier super-power formula. Once they realize these three countries have it, everyone will need to have theirs as well to keep up. It's the future of warfare—my product, my weapon. And it will make me the richest and most powerful woman on the planet. Just you wait and see."

I stared at her and her eyes seemed crazier than ever. "And then what?" I asked. "You have a family, remember? You have children. You're about to start another world war, is that what you want your children to grow up in? A world of war?"

"We're already at war," she hissed at me, spitting out champagne. "Don't you see that? Everyone thinks the next world war will be a cyberwar or a biological war sending out viruses to hurt your enemies. But no hacker and no virus can stop my super soldiers. They can march right in behind enemy lines and cause the necessary havoc. They can spy through the sewers; they can stop drone airplanes in the sky and blow up cities. I have created the perfect soldiers."

"And the creatures you extracted the DNA from? Where are they now?" I asked. "Won't you risk running out of material once you start to export it?"

Lisa laughed and shook her head. "Oh, I have more than enough. I need so little of their blood to create the serum. And soon, I'll start breeding them. Maybe even crossbreed several species. That would make for even more complex soldiers. The possibilities are endless."

She stared at me; her nose turned toward the sky. I knew that everything I was, even the way I looked, was appalling to her. I was everything she never wanted to be, everything she fought so hard not to become. I could tell in the way she stared at me. She grabbed my cheek and pulled it.

"One day, all people on earth will be genetically modified,

and we'll no longer have anyone like you running around. No one will be feeble; no one will be out of control like you are."

"Me? Out of control?" I asked. "That's hilarious coming from you."

She leaned forward and put her face close to mine. "I'm changing humanity, making it better, ridding it of weaklings like you. They'll put up statues of me all over the world and pay tribute to me. No more annoying stubby people like you, who can't seem to get their lives together or even stop eating when clearly it's time. No more millennials who can't even get to work on time and feel entitled to everything. People won't be WRONG all the time. They won't make mistakes constantly.

"Look around you. It's like people aren't even trying anymore. Everyone is so wrong all the time; no one is perfect anymore. No one even strives to be. But soon, it'll be over for good. People will be strong, people will be well, and they'll all love me for how I changed everything. People will listen to me when I speak."

"You truly are mad," I said. "How did you become like this? What the heck happened to you?"

Lisa let go of my cheek and turned her back to me, then drank her champagne.

"I lost a child once," she said, her voice suddenly low. "Only three days old."

My eyes grew wide. "I'm sorry, Lisa. I didn't know that."

"Spare me your pity. It was my fault. She was sleeping on her stomach when I went to check on her. I had put her down in the wrong position. I hadn't checked in on her. I am to blame for what happened. I made the mistake. I have to live with that. But I will never make a mistake again. Soon, people will stop making mistakes once I rid the world of normal people, don't you see?"

I see that you're stark raving mad, yes.

Lisa leaned over and caressed my cheek. "Faulty people like

you will be history, Emma. Everyone will be perfect, and no more babies will die. That's my legacy to the world. You're welcome."

"I didn't say thank you," I said and pulled away.

Lisa growled. "You don't understand anything. But that's okay. You don't have to. I see the bigger picture here. And now, I'll get rid of you as a gift to this new and perfect world."

She grabbed the gun from the guard, then placed it on my forehead.

"Wait," I said.

She lowered the gun.

"Can I at least see my children one last time? You know to say goodbye?" My voice was trembling as I spoke, and it was a struggle to get the words across my lips.

She stared down at me, the gun in her hand. Then she smiled.

Even her smile came off as manic, the way her upper lip vibrated. "I guess I could allow that. For old times' sake. It is, after all, not your fault you're so disgustingly flawed."

SEVENTY-FOUR

She took me to the lab. We walked in through the back entrance and up the stairs to the third floor, where she took me inside. I had to stop and catch my breath when I saw it. Inside were these huge cages made of clear material, looking like glass, but I guessed it was something way stronger if it was to keep the creatures locked up behind it.

There were so many of them, so many amazing creatures that I had no idea even existed. They all looked at me with dead and hopeless eyes as I walked past them, not even mustering enough courage to knock on the windows or scream for help.

I saw Daniel in a tank of water, and he had that same expression, yet when he saw me, his eyes lit up inside the liquid, and a hand appeared that touched the window. Yet, I could tell he knew I wasn't there to save him. I was a prisoner just like he was.

I swallowed and tried to smile at him, to induce some hope into him, but Lisa pulled me away. As we walked down the huge hallway, I spotted another familiar face.

Skye!

I rushed to her cage, then placed a hand on the window.

She was sitting in a fetal position, all curled up, and didn't look up until I put my hand on the window.

"Skye!" I said.

She looked up but didn't smile. Her eyes were pained and filled with despair.

"She has a way with your son," Lisa said. "It's proven to be very useful. As soon as we threaten to hurt the girl, your boy becomes like butter."

"You gave him her DNA, didn't you? When Victor first came to Fishy Pines, you started giving it to him. That's why he suddenly could do all those things, like make spoons levitate and speak to her in his mind."

Lisa nodded. "Victor is very special to us. He was the first real breakthrough we had in transferring the genetic material to humans. His body was very receptive and reacted right away."

"The blood," I said. "His blood turned dark green. I did wonder why I hadn't seen it before."

"Yes, it was truly amazing. We knew he was very special when he exploded the windows in the classroom at Fishy Pines. It was so soon after we had started the treatment altering his DNA code that it left us baffled. The things he was suddenly capable of, like creating fireballs between his hands and exploding things with his mind. In him, we combined the girl's powers and later added the freeze powers from our frost friend over there," Lisa said and pointed at a creature behind a wall of clear plastic, covered in white frost. His skin was blue, his lips purple, and his nails like icicles. He was gorgeous.

"That gave Victor the powers to freeze and explode the drone plane you saw outside," Lisa continued. "It makes him the most valuable test subject we have right now. The North Koreans want him, but I'm not sure they have enough money in the world, to be honest. I might keep him here and try to add more strength and power to him, make him invincible. You don't need to worry about him when you're gone. He's going to be fine. I'll make sure of that."

I forced a smile but felt my eye twitch.

"He's right over here if you want to say goodbye now," Lisa said. "But make it fast. I don't have all night."

I saw my son sitting behind a window, then ran to him. I placed a hand on the plastic, and he looked up at me from behind his curls.

"Victor. Victor, are you all right?"

He nodded. I sighed with relief. He seemed to be in great shape, physically at least. A tear escaped my eye while Lisa grabbed my shoulder.

"That's enough."

I wiped the tear away with my hand and turned to face her. "And my daughter? What about Maya?"

SEVENTY-FIVE

"She's asleep. You can't see her now. I've had enough of this. It's getting old."

Maya opened her eyes and looked in the direction of the sound. She had heard her name mentioned and was certain it was her mother's voice. She tried to move in the bed but was strapped down so tightly. Next to her, they had prepared some kind of liquid that they were pumping into her through a drip that was hooked into her shoulder. It made her feel sick and nauseated.

"M-mom?" she said. "MOM? I'm here. MOM?"

The voices grew agitated, and there was a fight of some sort, but seconds later, she heard her mother's voice again.

"Maya, sweetie. My baby?"

She opened her eyes again and looked into her mother's, then smiled with the little strength she had.

Her mom was there all right, looking at her.

"Mom? Mom? Have you come to take me out of here? I just want to go home. Can we go home now?"

"Oh, sweetie. What are they doing to you?"

Maya was about to speak when the awful woman, the one

in charge whom she had heard yell at the doctors often, and they all feared and spoke to with trembling voices, came up behind her mother.

"Mom. Careful, she's behind you."

Maya's mom acted fast. She leaned forward and hugged Maya tightly, then whispered in her ear.

"Be ready. We're getting out of here. You hear me?"

Maya cried as the woman, who was also the mayor, grabbed her mother from behind and pulled her away from Maya.

"Mom! Don't go, please. I need you! Mom! MOM!"

She cried as her mother was dragged down the hallway by the mayor with the help of a guard.

Her mother was screaming her name.

"MAYA!"

"Mom! Please, don't hurt her, please!"

Maya cried, her chest heaving up and down as she hyperventilated when she suddenly felt like the strap around her chest became looser. She looked down, then moved her arms and shoulders and noticed that it had been unstrapped.

Maya's eyes grew wide.

Mom did this. She must have done it when she hugged me!

Maya moved a little more, and soon she was able to get herself free, then sit up and pull the drip out of her shoulder. She had to regain composure as she felt dizzy at first, but seconds later, she was able to set her feet on the floor and stand up. In the distance, she could hear her mother screaming, but she knew the mayor or at least the guard would be armed. She was no match for either of them.

Maya turned on her heel and looked at the cages in front of her.

She wasn't armed. But others were.

SEVENTY-SIX

"Maya!"

I screamed at the top of my lungs as Lisa shoved me down the hallway. She grabbed me by the hair, then dragged me forcefully across the floor while I yelled my daughter's name. I didn't know if I had succeeded in opening her strap or not, but I prayed it would work.

"Please, Lisa, you don't want to do this," I said as she finally let go of me, and I sank to the ground. "Please. I am a mother. You are a mother. Think of your children. Once they know what you've done, Lisa, it'll crush them."

She punched me in the face. "Shut up. Stop talking now."

I fell to the floor, my nose bleeding, feeling woozy. My head had taken a lot of blows these past few days.

I watched through blurry eyes as Lisa approached a tube of some sort, then opened it.

"W-what is that?" I asked.

Lisa grabbed me by the armpits, then dragged me toward it. I was out of it at this point—dizzy and confused, unable to muster any resistance.

"When we test our subjects, we have to expose them to

extreme conditions in order to know how they'll react once they're out there. This one exposes them to extreme heat."

She put me on the floor of it, then walked out, and before I could get up, she closed the door. I looked at her, then knocked on the sides.

"Hey, let me out of here."

I watched her push some buttons on the sides, then straighten her hair before she looked at me.

"There. At least you won't be cold anymore."

"Lisa. Let me out of this thing. It's getting really hot in here. Lisa!"

But she didn't bother concerning herself with me any longer. She turned her back to me, then walked away.

I stared after her, then felt how I quickly began to sweat heavily. It was running down my forehead, and my hands became clammy. Soon, my shirt was soaked, and I felt faint. I sat down, trying to breathe properly. Every breath felt like fire in my lungs as the hot air entered me and scorched my insides on the way down.

I wanted to get up and fight for my life, but I couldn't. Instead, I was on all fours, panting heavily while struggling to stay awake. Finally, I couldn't hold myself up anymore.

I sank to the floor, face-first, and swam into the unknown.

SEVENTY-SEVEN

When Ingrid saw Maya's face outside the door to her cage, she couldn't help but smile. The last time she had seen this girl was in the alley when Ingrid decided to run away from what she had done.

Now, she was outside her cage, fumbling with the lock, tapping in numbers.

"I don't know the code," she grumbled. "I can't open it without the right code!"

That made Ingrid smile even wider. She had seen it being tapped in enough times to know. She had hoped to be able to use it one day but had never thought she would.

"It's the same on all of the cages," she said. "Three-one-twelve, the date Lisa Rasmussen's baby died. March first, twenty twelve. I heard her tell a guard one day."

"Three-one-twelve," Maya repeated, then tapped the numbers in, and the lock clicked. Never had Ingrid heard a sweeter sound in her life.

"It worked," Maya said, then pulled the handle and opened the door. Ingrid sprang out. She wanted to hug Maya but was terrified she might accidentally freeze her, so she didn't.

"Thank you," Ingrid said instead.

"We need to save my mom," Maya said. "Can you help me with that? I saw that woman drag her down the hallway. I think she wants to kill her."

Ingrid nodded. "Let's go then."

They ran down the hallway, while the many creatures in the cages started knocking on the sides as they realized Ingrid had been released. She yelled at Maya to stay back and get them out while she took care of her mother. She only risked getting hurt if she came with her anyway. Maya agreed, and Ingrid continued. She ran down another hallway and took a left, hoping it was the right direction.

It was.

She found Emma Frost inside a tube with the heater turned on. Emma was slumped on the floor and looked lifeless.

Am I too late? Please, don't let me be too late.

She started tapping on the buttons on the side when a voice came up behind her.

"I wouldn't do that if I were you," she said.

Ingrid turned around and saw Lisa Rasmussen approaching, a gun in her hand. She aimed it at Ingrid, then fired.

Instinctively Ingrid lifted her hand and froze the bullet as it left the barrel. The bullet fell to the floor, covered in a block of ice.

"You taught me that, remember?" Ingrid said triumphantly. She stepped forward toward Lisa, who fired the gun again, then again. Ingrid removed each and every bullet using her freeze powers, laughing. Seeing this, Lisa panicked. She threw the gun at her, then took off running.

Thinking she'd have to deal with her later, Ingrid turned to Emma and tapped the code into the side of the tube. The door clicked, and she opened it. A wave of excruciating heat hit her and almost melted the frost off her. But being as cold as she was turned out to be an advantage because she could walk inside without any issues, barely sensing the extreme heat. She grabbed Emma in her arms, then carried her out of the tube and put her on the floor. Then she hugged her and held her tight, trying to cool her down quickly.

"Come on, Emma. Please, wake up. Please."

SEVENTY-EIGHT

I was so hot; it felt like I was on fire. As I slowly came to, I suddenly felt a wave of coolness. It was rushing in over me, putting out the excruciating fire inside me, and soon I opened my eyes. The first thing I saw was a young girl wrapped around me, hugging me tightly.

"W-who are you?" I asked.

Realizing I had woken up, she let go. "Emma Frost, you're alive."

"Yes, indeed, I am. And who are you? Have I seen you before?"

"I'm Ingrid. I've been living in your basement."

"You've been living in my basement? We were looking for you. You were the one who killed the guy from Fishy Pines and tried to stop them from getting rid of that girl's body. Maya saw you."

"Yes, that was me. But there's no time for that now. We can talk and explain more later."

She helped me get to my feet, and I looked around. Seeing this, Ingrid guessed I was looking for my daughter.

"Maya is helping to release everyone," she said. "She's the one who let me out first. I promised to help you."

I smiled.

"It worked," I said with a sigh of relief. "And what about Lisa Rasmussen, the mayor?"

Ingrid looked toward the doorway. "She ran away just before I pulled you out."

I glanced at the doorway, then at Ingrid. "We need to get her. She can't get away. Quick."

SEVENTY-NINE

Lisa was pressing her ear against the door of the restroom. She had run in there to hide when that girl had attacked her with ice. She hadn't quite expected to have to be the one confronting her and shooting at her had been her only option, even though she knew the girl would use her powers to stop the bullets. Of course, she would. But what else could she have done?

Dang it.

Things weren't progressing exactly the way Lisa wanted them to right now. And it annoyed her. Why couldn't people just stop doing the wrong things? Why couldn't they just stop messing with her and see how wonderfully perfect it all was?

People are stupid; that's why.

It was the truth. There were so many stupid people in this world, especially the times lived in now. Social media had exposed them all and their stupidity.

No one thinks big anymore, and when they do, it's frowned on. What has this world come to?

She could hear voices approaching and realized one of them belonged to Emma Frost, the most annoying woman in the world. The girl had to have released her somehow, and now they were looking for Lisa. She could hear them saying her name. Lisa had locked the door and hoped they wouldn't try to look for her in the restroom.

She listened carefully as the voices were right outside the door, and she held her breath.

That's it. Keep going. Look for me everywhere except in the restroom. Who would be so silly as to hide out here when trying to escape, right?

"We have to find her before she gets away," she heard Emma Frost say.

"But the place is enormous," another voice said.

It sounded like the girl, the one who froze everything. Lisa had been so proud of her during the demonstration. Think of the gift she had given her. And this was how she thanked her.

The world was nothing but ungrateful idiots.

"You try that way; I'll go down the stairs," Emma Frost said.

"What about in there?" the girl asked.

"I don't think she's stupid enough to hide in the restroom," Emma Frost said.

Lisa giggled inside herself. Emma was too easy to fool.

A noise coming from one of the toilets behind her made her turn and look.

What was that? It sounded like a thump.

Lisa shook her head. It didn't happen again, so she put her ear back against the door.

"Try to go down that hallway," Emma Frost said.

Yes, try that hallway. Then I'll sneak out and use the fire escape while you search everywhere else for me. You make it almost too easy for me, Emma. You'll never learn, will you?

Another thumping, almost banging noise coming from behind her made Lisa turn and look. But nothing was there. Just the stalls with their toilets and the sinks outside, hanging on the wall.

My mind is playing tricks on me. That's all it is. Ignore it, and it'll go away on its own.

Lisa closed her eyes, trying to block out the noise, but as she opened them, it was even louder than before.

EIGHTY

The world was spinning, and it was hard for me to think straight. I knew Dr. Williamsen would be so angry with me right now for running around the way I was when I had a concussion, but I saw no other way. I had to stop Lisa before she made it out of here... before she disappeared.

Maya had released all the creatures, and they were helping to search. Victor and Skye were in each other's arms, not letting go of each other. I wondered if they ever would. It was kind of cute.

"Mom, I'm going with you."

Maya came up behind me, just as I had sent Ingrid down a hallway. I was about to walk to the stairwell when I stopped to wait for her. I turned to look at my gorgeous daughter, feeling relieved that I had saved her from the mayor's long claws.

And that was when I heard it. A loud thumping and banging noise.

"What was that?" Maya asked. She was walking toward me but stopped.

"It's like it's coming from inside the walls."

My eyes grew wide as I looked at her. I knew this sound a

little too well. I reached out my arm just as Maya was about to walk closer.

"No! Stay back!"

But Maya was already walking in front of the door, and as the noise grew louder, almost deafening, I threw myself at her, pushing her away from the door.

"It's not the walls; it's the pipes!" I yelled as I landed on top of her. "It's water!"

The next second, the door exploded, and a huge wave of water gushed out, flushing with it the one person we had all been looking for.

Lisa Rasmussen.

EPILOGUE

Morten scratched his forehead. He had been doing that a lot while I explained to him—for the fifth time—what had happened at the lab. Luckily, I had witnesses now to tell him I wasn't some crazy lady making up silly stories. A bunch of them were guards who had spilled the beans on Lisa and were more than willing to cooperate with the police.

And now, as he stared at the many creatures walking around in the lab, talking, hugging, high-fiving one another, he knew it was true. Everything I had babbled about was true, and even to me, that was quite strange.

"So, you're telling me the water creature…"

"Lyn," I said, nodding. "Daniel's mom."

"Yes, all right, she came through the pipes and flushed Lisa Rasmussen out."

"She came right on time," I said and nodded at her. She was with Daniel, who hadn't left her side since she flushed out of the bathroom. I was so grateful that she showed up right when we needed it.

"And let me get that part about the freeze powers again;

how did they give them to the people they kidnapped from the island?"

I sighed and explained it all again. I couldn't blame him for finding it hard to understand. Lisa Rasmussen was in custody and had been taken away in cuffs. I just hoped the police would be able to find a way to put her away for life. I had a feeling the fingerprints on the ice pick that killed Finnerup would be enough. It was a case that we could actually take to court. None of us believed any judge would believe the rest of the story.

Maya came up behind me and hugged my neck, then whispered in my ear. "I think it's time."

"Time?" Morten asked. "For what exactly?"

I turned to look at the strange creatures, one more magnificent than the next.

"They need to go home," I said. "Lyn told me she found the entrance. She's been looking for it, but apparently, it was blocked off by a brick wall that was built back in the eighties when the creatures were first pulled out of the pipes at Fishy Pines. And that's why they couldn't get back.

"Samuel, the old vampire, was the first to come to the island that way more than a hundred years ago, and since then, many more arrived after him, most of them back in the eighties when their world was ravaged by a devastating war. But they need to go home, Morten. They don't belong here. They'll always be in danger from people like Lisa, I am afraid. We're not ready for them. Maybe we never will be."

Morten nodded. He was still pale and had that look of extreme confusion in his eyes. I couldn't blame him. It was a lot to take in at once.

"All right. Let's send them home then and put an end to all this."

. . .

It was with great worry that I watched Morten and his colleagues open the door to the condemned part of the Fishy Pines building. I was sad to see all my new friends go, yet still happy they would go back to where they belonged and where they wouldn't be treated as experiments.

But I was sad to see Skye leave, and I hadn't talked to Victor about it. They were holding hands and rushed into the old hallways as the door was opened, going along with all the other creatures. In some fashion, it felt like Victor was more at home with these people than here in our world. And I feared he felt that way too.

The fear became a reality once we came to the place where Lyn said the opening was. It was in the basement, down where the sewers of the town were. It was dusty and dirty in there, but it was very obvious the brick wall in front of us wasn't as old as the rest.

With a huge sledgehammer, Morten knocked some of the bricks loose, and a strong wind suddenly blew in, bringing smells of trees and plants with it. *Somewhere on the other side was another world*, I thought, then looked at the people around me. *Their world.*

I looked down at my son, who had come up next to me and grabbed my hand. The look in his eyes broke my heart in more ways than I can describe. I swallowed to be able to speak because of the giant knot growing in my throat.

"Y-you want to go with them, don't you?"

Saying the words crushed me inside, but I had to say it. I felt it just as strongly as he did.

Victor nodded. Of course, he did. Skye was his greatest love, and, in many ways, he was so much more like all these people than he was like me. Especially now that his DNA had been altered, and we didn't know if it was going to last the rest of his life. He belonged in a place like that.

"All right," I said. "But after you're gone, they'll close the wall up again. You won't be able to come back."

He nodded, then grabbed my hand in his. "I know, Mom. Don't worry about me."

I actually didn't. I worried more about myself. How was I supposed to live without him?

"We'll take care of him for you," Lyn said, coming up behind Victor. "He can live with us. He and Daniel are good friends already."

I sniffled, pressing back tears. I couldn't believe this was happening. I had just gotten my son back, and now I was saying goodbye to him. But on the other hand, he had these new powers that I feared would make people want to do experiments on him again. He was still a valuable weapon, and our world wasn't ready for someone like him.

Letting him go was also protecting him.

It just didn't feel good.

I knelt in front of him, and he lifted his gaze and looked into my eyes.

"Bye, Mom. I love you."

Then he hugged me. He hadn't done that in years, and the sensation it left me with stayed with me for a long time after I had waved at him, and he had walked hand in hand with Skye into the pipes.

As soon as I couldn't see him anymore, I fell to my knees and cried. Maya grabbed me and escorted me back, while Morten and his colleagues sealed up the entrance again.

Once back in the hallways of Fishy Pines, I grabbed my daughter in my arms and cried, shaking so badly that both she and I trembled.

"It's gonna be okay, Mom," she said. "He's a big boy now. It was right of you to let him make the decision himself. It's gonna be tough for a little while, but we'll all be happy we did eventually."

I looked at her. My beautiful, wonderful daughter was trying to make me feel better, even though I could tell she was falling apart inside herself.

"How am I supposed to live without him? How?" I asked.

She shook her head. "I... I don't..."

"You don't have to."

I let go of Maya and turned around. In the doorway stood my Victor. He wasn't looking at me but had his hair in front of his eyes as usual. Yet, he was smiling.

"Victor? Victor?" I shrieked. "But..."

"I changed my mind," he said and approached me. "I want to stay here. Maybe I'll go when I'm an adult. But not now."

Morten came out after him, panting. "He just jumped out right when we were about to seal it off."

I grabbed the boy in my arms, then kissed his hair and face excessively until he told me to stop and walked away. I was crying rivers as I looked at my son, happy to get to experience him growing up after all. Then I felt an arm around my shoulder, and Morten pulled me into a hug.

"I'm not letting you go either," he whispered in my ear. "Ever again. Do you hear me? We belong together. We'll just have to figure out the rest."

I sniffled and let the tears roll down my cheeks, and he grabbed my chin and pulled me into a kiss.

In the background, the kids made annoying noises, and Maya told us to get a room.

Everything was the way it was supposed to be.

Back to normal.

I laughed and wiped my tears away, then walked arm in arm with Morten out of Fishy Pines and into the parking lot, where they were putting police tape up to signal that the place was closed. All the kids would be sent home to their families.

HP had been arrested at his home that same night and promised to cooperate with the police, Morten told me. So far, he had admitted they were trying to get rid of the girl's body in the alley but that he acted on orders from Finnerup and Lisa. He had also told them that the girl was a patient and agreed to give them the parents' information so they could be contacted. It was quite a mess that needed to be cleaned up over the next few months, but luckily, it wasn't my mess.

My responsibilities were with Maya and Victor for now. Maya had asked if Alex could come live with us because both his parents were dead, and he had no place to live, and I had agreed as long as they had separate bedrooms and stayed in them at night. If I found him in her bed, I'd have him out of there, pronto.

Ingrid had gone back to her parents' house, but before she left in the police car taking her home, she promised to come to visit me from time to time. She and Victor shared something amazing, and I had a feeling they might strike up a friendship.

I happily thought this when I felt the car keys leave my hand, and they hung in the air in front of me, then shot through the air, where Victor grabbed them with a huge grin, then ran to open the car.

As I said, everything was back to normal. As normal as it got on this weird island, at least.

A LETTER FROM WILLOW

Dear Reader,

I want to say a huge thank you for choosing to read *Black Frost*. If you enjoyed it and want to keep up to date with all my latest releases, just sign up at the following link. Your email address will never be shared, and you can unsubscribe at any time.

www.bookouture.com/willow-rose

I hope you loved *Black Frost* and if you did, I would be very grateful if you could write a review. I'd love to hear what you think, and it makes such a difference helping new readers to discover one of my books for the first time.

As always, I want to thank you for all your support and for reading my books. I love hearing from my readers—you can get in touch through social media or my website, or email me at madamewillowrose@gmail.com.

Take care,

Willow

KEEP IN TOUCH WITH WILLOW

www.willow-rose.net

facebook.com/willowredrose

x.com/madamwillowrose

instagram.com/willowroseauthor

bookbub.com/authors/willow-rose

PUBLISHING TEAM

Turning a manuscript into a book requires the efforts of many people. The publishing team at Bookouture would like to acknowledge everyone who contributed to this publication.

Commercial
Lauren Morrissette
Hannah Richmond
Imogen Allport

Cover design
The Brewster Project

Data and analysis
Mark Alder
Mohamed Bussuri

Editorial
Jennifer Hunt
Sinead O'Connor

Proofreader
Joni Wilson

Milton Keynes UK
Ingram Content Group UK Ltd.
UKHW011432140724
445326UK00004B/135

9 781835 253458